A TALE OF ANCIENT EGYPT

A TALE OF ANCIENT EGYPT

FREDERICK C. HECKEL

PHILOSOPHICAL LIBRARY

New York

PRINTED IN THE UNITED STATES OF AMERICA

CONTENTS

CHAPTER I

Up the River of Time

To us, a journey to the past suggests old palaces, half-ruined temples with a few old priests chanting strange words that they themselves no longer can rightly comprehend. "Past" means, the dead past, living, if at all, a ghostly half-life.

Hard is it for the twentieth century man to think of any past time as a vibrant, young time, filled and over-filled with energies of life, restless and errant, wanting things to do yet far from sure of what its true task is.

Yet so I found the life of Ancient Egypt. In many ways it was akin to ours, and they blood brothers to us who dream of visiting the stars in space ships launched from great earth-satellites. And still, and still, they were a different breed, those men of Khem, the land of the black earth. The stars, for them, were neighbors closer by than Asia, say, to the average Western Man. The stars were the homes of godhead. Men's souls, they held, could visit stars at night. slipping from the body left behind on earth. And Divine Visitors went among earth people.

This last was why my own arrival made no such great stir, and why I was not killed on sight when I appeared among the local troops guarding the Southern Borders. First, the machine in which I was took shape before them—a metallic gleaming that quickly resolved itself into a disk-like wheel, flat on the edges, high enough in the middle for a sitting man.

When I then raised the port and stood at my full height before them I realized that my six feet one was the advantage we had hoped it would be. For none of them came near to me in tallness. So too my blond skin and light hair proved a good passport to the awed respect of these dark soldiers. My pale-

1

ness confirmed, for them, my apparent unearthly origin. Otherwise I would have been most swiftly killed as a violator of the border.

Posted as guard against the incursions of black-skinned raiders from the South, these young men, dark themselves yet in no way negroid, were an outpost of about twenty all told. Servants of the Lord of Elephantine, they prostrated themselves now before the strange white figure that loomed taller still by reason of the shining disk on which he stood.

I had to speak, and now the great problem rose. For modern men, quite capable of deciphering the written words of Egypt, have had, until my return, no accurate comprehension of how these words were spoken, how pronounced.

Yet something must be ventured, and I drew a deep breath and spoke. The scholars—and we had limited the number of those told of our plan, for reasons obvious enough—the savants had given me their best advice. They taught me to say a few words as they thought, without any assurance, was the way the men of old had spoken them. And for many days and nights before the journey I had repeated, so I could say them in my dreams, a few sentences:

"Im Hotep, Im Hotep, in peace, in peace. I come great distances and am not familiar with the speech of Khem, but prepared am I to learn it."

I used them now, making my voice as full and resonant as possible. I repeated them, with a slightly different intonation. The young captain, who had maintained his place before the unbroken rank of his little company—this itself an act of courage, as his men showed courage too in just maintaining their formation, which will become clear enough if you think yourself into their position facing an unearthly stranger—the young captain raised his head from the ground after my third repeating.

"Hotep an ka, peace to you," he responded.

I smiled, and raised my arms and held them toward him, curved like the hieroglyph that means to embrace.

"Who art thou?"

"A man of this same earth but of a far time," I answered.

To you who read my account, this might seem strange. Why

2

spoil the advantage to be derived from any childlike idea that a god stood before them?

But the planners had been unanimous, and I with them, that full adherence to the simple (and sometimes not-so-simple) truth must be my constant course. In the first place we knew, as all scholars know, that these were *not* a childlike people. If our mathematics and physics had been sound, and the machine rightly set, I had arrived at the unfolding time in Egypt —the time of the Great Builders of the Great Pyramids. It was then that the lasting patterns that were to hold a civilization upright for well past two thousand years were themselves being created, were being shaped from the youthful will of mighty men.

Meanwhile behind these strong and youthful leaders there already lay a thousand and a half a thousand years of vivifying growth of the two Kingdoms, Upper Egypt walled in its narrow valley and Lower Egypt spread into the Delta and open to the entire Mediterranean World. *The Calendar,* true and accurate and the direct ancestor of our own, had been worked out by the astronomers of the Delta Cities more than fifteen hundred years before. And a culture that could do that was no land of little children. And now for several hundred years already the Kingdoms had been united and been groping towards the development of the Great Century in which everything seemed, literally, to come into being at once.

There was another, and even stronger, consideration for adhering to the truth. These Men of Egypt strove to live by TRUTH. MAAT, they called her. Daughter she was of the Sun God Ra, Himself, and bearer of the food by which the world of the Gods was sustained. Had they lived by Maat? In essence this was what all men were judged on in the Halls of Osiris after earthly death. And in truth I soon found that already here on earth, in this life, they were judged by the same standard.

It was not just a technical abiding by the Truth. The thing went further. It amounted to a shaping of one's whole life by the underlying laws of rightness, the laws of cosmic harmony that keep the planets in their proper paths. The Men

3

of Khem, I was to learn, had long since realized that these same laws of Truth, of dynamic balance in the Heavens, underlie the life and functioning of everything on this earth planet. But enough of this for now.

The captain only half believed my disclaimer of divinity, not taking it as a lie, but rather a display of godly courtesy. He was most respectful and invited me to come with him to visit his ruler, the Lord of Elephantine.

He seated me amidships in a little boat woven of Nile reeds tied in bundles, rising at either end to give the suggestion of a crescent moon. Light in weight it was, and it had been lying on the bank. Already it was almost dried out since its last use earlier that day. Two servants carried it easily down a sloping beach and set it in the water, holding it while I stepped aboard and seated myself. The young man got in after me but remained standing. The servant at the upstream end held fast the stern while the other let go and went back up the bank to bring two paddles.

With these they guided us diagonally out across the river, both paddling on the downstream side, enough to keep us on our course to the landing on the East Bank about a quarter of a mile below the island.

I was struck by the gracefulness with which they did their work. Angular in a sense, their movements were—as seen by my mid-twentieth-century eyes. Yet there was nothing in the sharp-edged motions that savored in any way of the mechanical. Their active bodies flowed.

At the same time I had the first of an endless series of inner experiences that I can, perhaps, transmit to you who read this. To the men of Khem, even when I had learned their speech to the extent of struggling with ideas—picture-ideas they had to be or they meant nothing—I never could convey what I was feeling: tears, genuine tears would come to my eyes to see, turned to motion, a picture I had so often looked at in the wall reliefs and paintings. Here on my little ship of straw the rowers on the Nile, from being frozen into stone and ancient pigment, came into life and movement.

You may say: "But the fellahin, the poor peasantry left in

4

that ancient land in our own time, still handle their little boats in the same way." In a sense that is true enough, but what is gone forever is the zest, the life in what they do.

This held for everything, the land workers in their rhythms in the yearly round of field work, the potters at their wheels, the herdsman carrying a calf across his shoulders as he forded an irrigating ditch with his cows behind him.

All of you, born in this modern day, who have in them a love for the things of Ancient Egypt, will understand what I mean. The "scientific" side of what I found in those months of my journey back in time, all of that, the food for scholars, will appear in due course in the learned publications that those who sent me are, in their unhurried way, preparing with my aid. Their reluctance, their hesitation to take my word, the cross-examinations I have now become accustomed to—these things are touching, and yet understandable, for so many theories must fall.

On the opposite side of the stage from the scholars, there stood for awhile the public, frenzied by the first news reports that they wanted to disbelieve but could not. These have mostly fallen away and concern themselves with the latest great sensation. And that too is good. For thus it comes about that we, who have a bond in our love of all the things of that ancient place and time, are left relatively undisturbed to consider them together.

I must resume the telling of my journey to the Nomarch, that powerful lord who already waited in his hall of audience, having been informed of strange events, by one who was sent when I first had made trial of their speech. But one thing I must first explain.

A little space back I made a disclaimer of being, myself, one of the scientists whose lives are given to the study of this old river kingdom and her people.

"Why, then, did they send you?" my readers may well be asking. Answering here I have need to affirm my respect for those dedicated scholars. When the physicists came and told them they had made the machine that was capable of movement back in time, they said that they themselves would not be qualified to make the observations that alone could justify the venture. They asked the Egyptologists to nominate the one who should go. So then these men—I repeat, there were only a few who knew the secret beforehand, but these were the best in their field—these men, after long discussions, decided that they too were not qualified to go. This on the very grounds of all their learning. They realized that, filled as they were with the best knowledge of our time concerning those great years of Egypt, they would be incapable of fresh, objective observation unhindered by pre-judgments. So they chose me, whom you, my readers, know of as a traveler in strange places whose reports, though full of a joy in what he saw, a love of the peoples he met, have yet always been as true and accurate as he could make them. This at the same time that the tales I have brought back make no claim to being "scientific data."

We reached the audience chamber of the Keeper of the Southern Gate, my little, dark captain and I. He prostrated himself. I bowed respectfully but kept my feet firm on the cool tiles.

"Say to me, thou art of the Gods, and I will worship." These were the first words he spoke, and I caught enough of them to be able to smile and to answer.

"I, like thee, am a man of this earth," I responded, "but out of another time, brought here by a wisdom men have wrested, for good or ill, out of the lost Book of Thoth that held all wisdom."

"You have, I see, some knowledge of our tradition," the Nomarch answered, with just a trace of smiling, near his eyes.

From here on the interview was halting. My few stock phrases were all insufficient to cope with his perceptive questioning. I could only make clear my need of learning the language, and my eagerness to clarify the facts of my arrival when I could.

This was a most capable man whom the King of Egypt, Lord of the Two Lands, had placed at his Southern Gateway. The Nomarch had long since read in my obvious limitations and respectful hesitancies, that I was in truth no supernatural being, but a slightly frightened man.

I for my part could gather much, less from his words than out of that "understanding" that can leap, spark-wise, great gaps when any two people face each other on foundations of common humanity alone, not forgetting mutual good will. He felt that technically, and morally, by Maat, he was bound to send me by swift vessel down the river to the great Double Palace of the King, to be disposed of there by the King's will. Yet he was able to make clear to me that he would not do this.

"Much of value for mankind," he explained, "as well as for our own Initiates, will be lost in that way. I know the King's mind well. He is a harsh builder who erects, with power that has no room for tenderness, a One Great Land out of this Double Kingdom. And he lives by Maat in so doing. Alien influences are what he will not have. As you are now, stumbling and halting in your speech and in your comprehending of us, you would go Northward only to quick death. And this is still your likely ending, soon enough, in Khem. And yet I feel that the very Gods of Egypt—and believe me, pale stranger, these Gods not only live, but guide our land; I feel that our Gods desire it otherwise. I will give you for awhile to my Chief Scribe here, one named Imhotep after an early Great One."

He smiled again, for he saw I knew and had recognized that name.

"If your words are true," he continued (I can only paraphrase, but am confident I caught, already then, the essence of what he said). "If your words are true as to your origins, some things at least have journeyed too, in time, from out of Khem into the later ages.

"I give you to Imhotep. Learn our language diligently. I can only keep you safe here until the return of the messenger I send, with my report, to the Golden Horus, this same day. A waning and a waxing again of the moon. This is the longest it can be before he is here again, surely bearing with him the decree for your swift sending by the water road to the North."

I managed to make clear to him before whom I stood that it would be well if my machine were meantime guarded by his trusted servants night and day. He nodded and dismissed me.

"The service of the Horus King must be diligently attended, whatever strange things happen in a day," he said, half aloud. "I have reports of Nubians massing not far off."

There began for me then, weeks of concentrated study on which would depend, not just my life but my task, which was of far greater importance. And I was struck with wonder as to the skill with which our philologists, across the desert gulf of thousands of years, had done their reconstruction of the language of the Nile People.

Most of our work in those short weeks was with pronunciations. I had been well drilled in vocabulary and language structure, and I blessed those scholars who had labored on me, and those who, earlier, had made such a fantastic language study as I was undertaking possible.

CHAPTER II

I Glimpse Osiris

My schooling with Imhotep lasted almost the full four weeks the Nomarch had predicted. I had arrived on the first quarter of the moon. It was a few days short of this time when the messenger returned with the demand that my person be produced at the Great House.

"I will keep you by me until the moon sphere is again where it was on your arriving in our Valley," he said to me. "My swift ship and best rowers will bring you to Him soon enough. He will not chide me. And it is better, for you, that the rhythm be kept. These time cycles all have mighty meaning, for time is itself a kind of space in which the Gods swim and perform the deeds that they must do according to the will of the Great God."

I was to bless him later for his wisdom. It is due to the delay that I remained alive and was able to come back, unharmed to our time. Neither of us, of course, knew this then, at least not consciously.

I had learned, days ago, that we were in the reign of Khephren, that Great King known to modern man through his statue with the falcon, wings outspread, behind his head. This King, ruthless by our modern standards, was the second of the Three, the Great Architects of the living shape of Khem. Khufu, later called Cheops by the Greeks, had been the embodiment of Will. What had been begun by his forebear, Narmer, smiter of the rebellious, in uniting the Two Kingdoms, was inwardly carried through by the one who had built the first Great Pyramid. He had taken, and woven, the will of the Land into one will, his own.

9

Now Khephren, bearer of the force of Thinking, had patterned Wisdom, livingly, like delicate nerve fibers up and down the length of the great land. These thought-antennae lived in the persons of his Noble Servants, the Great Lords who did his will, scattered strategically from the Cataracts to the Delta Country where men watched always for invaders from the Sea.

And all the living nerve-fibers that were men, transmitted their impulses, as to a brain, to Khephren, Lord of the Wisdom. Priesthood and Rulership, I found, were united in these Lords. All had been trained as far as their capacities would take them, in the Wisdom of Egypt.

This wisdom, so different from what our later, modern mystics dreamed, had most to do with deeds for the transforming of the earth: that which we today would call engineering—hydraulics and irrigation, architecture and the science of transporting great building stones. The healing art was part of it, of course, and plant and cattle breeding. Pedagogy was highly evolved. In fact there was no field of human endeavor that was not priest-guided. And these same priests were the leaders and the doers. While with it all there was a humility that thrived in the knowledge that men *by themselves* could never have done all that which they accomplished.

They worshipped the Gods because they knew it was the Gods that worked through conscious man to do the deeds that would lead the human spirit's evolution on its proper path. These men saw their life as a kind of partnership with the Divine.

I bowed deeply, with genuine respect, yes, with reverence, before the Keeper of the Southern Gate when I left him, to board his swift vessel for my journey down the Nile. This was a great and wise man, though only one of many Lords of relatively equal rank. I shivered a little, dreading the standing face to face with the God-King to whom he was only a servant, though a loved and trusted one.

Now there came a time of great frustration for me. I traveled down the Nile in this great age of Ancient Egypt, yet saw nothing of the Land, and of the people only those that waited on me in my cabin.

10

He of Elephantine had explained it to me. The River, giver of life to the Land, was also a crowded highway. And it would not do to have me seen by Egypt's people.

Enough, in any case, would seep out to them concerning the pale stranger. Already tales were heard throughout the Nome. Thoth, the ibis-headed fisherman of thoughts, was masked as human, was visiting their Lord. And some said it was pale Khonsu, bearer of the life-engendering forces in the moon.

These things could not be avoided, and did no harm, he said. But as a servant of his Lord, the Great King, he had to keep a great abyss between this stranger and the people of Khem. Otherwise the power of Khephren, who was true man as well as a true Horus, would be weakened. Then he, the Keeper of the Southern Gate, would be held responsible, and rightly so.

"You speak of him to me as of a God?" I said, with the question implied in my tone.

The Nomarch smiled a little, and I smiled back, mis-reading him.

He shook his head.

"It is not, as your unschooled heart would tell you, imagery," he answered finally. "I perceive it is of no use, my trying to show you these things by speaking. In any case, for a long time or short, you shall experience these things in your own being. Then you will know my words are true.

"This much I am permitted to say, in warning. It is a great man, one of the world's ever-greatest Kings, before whom you will be bowing in the City of the White Wall. But do not be deceived to your own great cost. There dwells within that man, as in a noble palace, a powerful God whose thought, whose love, whose every deed is Egypt. He is the defender of his father, the Osiris Khufu, and of all that which belongs to his Father, the Glorified."

I had the wit to curb my tongue and take my leave in silence. I bowed deeply, not because court form demanded it, but out of respect for this man who, though he said things outside my comprehension had yet proven to me, many times over, his wisdom. And when I say *wisdom* I mean as I said

11

earlier nothing of that which Twentieth Century "mystics" mean when they use such a word. This Lord's wisdom was rather in being always one, of a piece with his task, not standing over against it as we moderns tend to do.

My unseeing voyage, rowed with oars aiding the force of the swelling Nile, was uneventful in the first days of it. I gathered from the captain that we bore some kind of pennant showing that we were on the Great King's business. Besides, he assured me, the swift ship of the Lord of the Southern Gate was herself well known as far as the White Wall. So we were never crowded, and could take the right of way even against the traffic coming upstream under sail, the ships that used the good wind blowing from the North.

At night we tied up by the bank. The captain saw to it that we stopped, always, in unfrequented places. And he kept armed guards patrolling a good perimeter of the shore, encircling us crescent-wise from beyond our bow to past the two great steering oars.

Yet the day before our arrival something strange developed, something that changed my fate entirely. Our ship was hailed, hailed by her own name, "King's Swift Falcon of the South, halt that I may speak to you."

Then I could hear the same voice, coming from beyond our starboard bows, giving commands to his crew, and to the helmsman. Sail was being furled on that great vessel.

"A ship of the Lord of the Double Crown," one of our crewmen muttered. Her sail was furled, and in a great sweep, carried by her momentum, she swung round and soon was fast beside us.

Our oars were inboard after the first hailing, and now the vessels drifted in the current.

"I must speak to your Lord," the other captain said. "In the name of the Gods that rule our land, lead me before him."

"I do not carry my Lord," our captain answered. "In his cabin there lies a prisoner of whom I am forbidden to speak to any save to the chamberlain of the great Double Palace by the White Wall."

12

There was a silence while the two shipmen appraised each other.

"And my message is only for the rulers of the districts," the other said, at last. "Depart, then, captain. To your ears I may not speak. May you come in, in peace, to the place where you go."

The ships cast loose from one another, and soon ours was again moving forward to the rhythm of the oars, down the middle of the Great River, ever nearer to the city Menes built.

My own curiosity was great, yet I, whose mission was to learn and to discover, had schooled myself never to ask a question where no question was invited. Mere prudence would have dictated this, the desire to be allowed to complete my task and return, through time, to the future that was my true home. But besides such considerations I already had, growing within me, transmitted to me from those with whom I was, a measure of the calmness, the attitude of waiting, that can only come from an inner sense of human dignity.

Strangely, and this I had not expected to be finding, this was no abstract feeling of the dignity of man but rather a true experiencing of the value of the individual. In an ordered, hierarchical, group-society this would seem to have been out of place. And yet, and yet, within the rigid form where, true enough, the individual meant nothing, there was, by the very nature of the relationship of man to man, a mutual respecting of the spark of Godhead that dwelt not only in greatest measure in the Priest-King, but lived also in the least of the servants of Him who in Himself *was* all of Egypt.

So I kept silent. And so, early in that night, when we were fast along a deserted stretch of the shore, beneath great cliffs (I could see them because at night I was allowed to walk about on the deck), the captain turned to me.

"I can only think," he said, in a low tone that others might not hear us, "I can only think it means that our Great King soon becomes an Osiris."

I stared at the captain, speechless at first.

"If your thought be true," I said at last, "then. . . ."

He caught my meaning.

"The Divine Prince," he answered, "is the Lord Menkare."

My heart beat faster with excitement, although I had known this was the Royal Successor. I held to calm of speech as we talked further of that young man, but my heart was light and glad, for I could have more hope now. Little enough was known of King Menkare, even by the servants of the King's servants. The Royal Line of Egypt, although they could be reached by those who appealed against judges' decisions, kept itself apart in certain ways from *all* men.

Herodotus, the Greek, two thousand years still in the future, knew, in some ways more of their kings than these men did. For the strange tales that grow, inevitably, around every leading personage of history, have always in their fantasy a core of hard reality carried with weird embellishments down the River of Time. And what Herodotus had said augured well for me. For all the stories, fantastic as they were, had one thing in common:

Menkare was another kind of being, was different from his two great predecessors, less great perhaps, but kind where they were cruel. I wondered, Oh I wondered if the captain's guess as to the change in rulership were right. And I had no way of knowing.

We came soon to the White Walled Memphis. Then our captain, probably out of pride in having been right—for certain human traits that we all know have not changed to a great degree in what is after all less than five thousand years—out of a pride in being right, I think it was, dared to depart from the literal command given him.

He came to the rear of the cabin.

"Part the hangings just a little," he said, "no one will see you, no one looks this way. Here is something in front of us that few, even of us river men, have ever seen."

It was the time of first light on the River. The sun had not yet risen over the cliffs far to the East, but the cloudless sky shone a very bright blue and the great city ahead of us on the right was clearly outlined in its multitude of buildings behind the bright, white wall that gave the place its name.

I had said "ahead of us" and this was true in relation to

our course, but the captain had beckoned to the hangings at the rear of the little cabin and it was from there that I was looking. He had turned the ship to head up-stream and the oarsmen just paddled enough to counteract the flow of the current and keep us in the same relative position with regard to the riverbanks. The sight astern—where all of the crew were looking with intentness—was one that might, at first glance, not have struck a modern man as remarkable.

A long traveling boat, of a dark wood, like our own, was putting out, solitary, from the quay, where a great fleet of such vessels waited. We were not near enough to see the figures on board with any distinctness. There was a great canopy, open at the sides. Under it something like a couch or bed, with a covered form stretched on it. Men stood around it, saying ritual words, and from the shore, dark with a multitude save for an area just by the landing, there came loud cries of mourning.

"The Great King goes, to become, now, an Osiris," the captain murmured softly.

I looked to the radiant East. The sun was appearing and sent level shafts of a golden light which, as it rose, illuminated that great vessel so that now it shone in sun-like beauty of its own.

"In the light she comes to greet him, to embrace him, Astet, the Isis, the sister-wife, the lady of heavenly wisdom," the voice murmured at my side. Then it seemed to me there *was* another presence on that ship with the dead King. I could not have explained it; I cannot now. Externally, it was only a good Nile vessel, alone on the great River, in mid-stream now and turning from us, departing faster as the oars bit in and her momentum grew. Yet it was more, unquestionably it was more.

It was the God-King who had laid aside his mortal part and was going to join the Company of the Gods.

"Put Neteru, the Company of the Gods," the captain murmured, as if he read the picture in my mind.

I happened to look into the sky, up over the ship that was departing. Strangely (I say "strangely" as I write this in *our* present, our here and now, though at the time it did not seem remarkable, simply due and proper), strangely, in

15

the sky directly over that dark vessel and soaring, with few wing-beats into the North Wind that blew cool from the distant sea, was a great hawk. That bird was alone in the sky as the ship was alone on the great River.

"What of these other ships along the shore?", I said at last.

The man who stood beside me, but on the open deck, gave a kind of convulsive start. It was as though my words had called him back into his body. He smiled a little, then.

"We still must wait, until they too are gone. Those are the Court, the highest nobles and the leaders of the priests of the whole Country. They go, after a decent interval, to follow their Lord to his River Temple on the West Bank. There the embalmers wait for him. There, with rituals that were ancient before Narmer made the Two Lands One and built the Great White Wall, his earthly body will be made eternal that he may revisit it when he desires.

"For you, O pale stranger, it portends a long waiting for the hearing of your fate. The Horus of Gold, the young defender of the rights of his Osiris Father, will at this same time be receiving his anointing. He will be taken as far into the mysteries as one who is still part mortal can, in this age of mankind, go. *He will become Egypt.*

"Yes," the man beside me shook his head, "there will be little left of that young King's Son of whom there are so many tales."

I was startled, and probably I showed this on my face, though I swear that in the cabin it was not light. Nor do I remember that at any time he had turned to look at me. So I was yet more startled at this man's next words.

"You wonder how a simple man, a river captain, can speak thus of his Lord, of his Lord that he knows to carry in himself essence of Godhood, and to whom his river captains belong as my hunting dogs belong to me.

"Now I *know* you are a man, as you claim to be. Else you would understand these things. You are no visitor from the Fields of Peace, NOR yet an emissary of Set, the Great Opponent, Lord of Midnight and all the Powers of Darkness. I will so report to the King's Chamberlain. And this, I believe, will be to your benefit, O Stranger.

"A good, a truthful heart, I find, too, in you." He laughed then. "You are not dead, nor I the Judge of the Dead or even his Doorkeeper. Though if any had heard me just now they might well have thought this.

"One word more. In your honest groping for Truth, you are become entitled to it. I can speak, in a certain way freely of my Lord because he IS Egypt and at the same time I, and all His People ARE Egypt too. Our tasks are different and yet the Great King needs me as he needs the least water-carrier there in that city, the least of the soldiers that guard his desert outposts. And we need him, as the blood that fills his body needs the kingly heart that it may receive from there sun-force that can re-enliven it."

"How come you by such knowledge, O River Captain?", I said finally.

The man smiled gently, pity in his eyes.

"Our earthly tasks are suited to our earth-capacities. And such labors are doubly good. For thus are men fed and provided for in their needs and the future of Khem made safe. At the same time they teach us what we need to learn—to enter deeper into life on Earth, not like our fathers' fathers and their fathers. They walked about and of a truth they knew the Gods. Yet their earth-waking was a dream while their dreams were a full awakeness.

"How come I by such knowledge, who am the humble servant of a servant?

"Good Stranger from a time that seems in truth to be god-forgotten, our priests, while leading us into the fields of Geb, the strong Earth Father, would not have us forget our Mother Nut, the Wise Lady clothed in stars. Each of us, even of low rank, is taught the meaning of as much as he still holds within his being of the great Ancient Wisdom that was common to all mankind long ago.

"We are dwellers in two worlds. We walk this earth without fear, without agitation because we know that we are never left alone for the wolves that prowl the borders of the soul world

17

to devour. Children must learn to walk without a hand extended to them. Yet the Elders stay near by.

"But enough. See, the fleet puts out now to follow the Great King on his way to his Shining Pyramid. We must come into harbor, that you may be delivered to those who wait for you."

The captain turned and gave commands to his men. For me, who had been allowed to look deep within him, it was as though I had again become a parcel of freight, a bale of cloth to be delivered. He, in his being, was as far from me as the being of any ship captain whose image I had looked at in a tomb painting in that future which now seemed so terrifyingly far back in my past.

Yet a thought had been born in my heart. Words of Scriptures still not written echoed in my inner self. Here had been, here was, Peace. Had the Bringer of Peace who was at the same time the Bringer of a Sword become lost to mankind because the meshes of their consciousness had become too coarse? I was determined to ask of these things in due time.

I had leisure for pondering, for as we drew near to the dockside the captain came back a moment and said to me that it would be necessary that I stay within my cubicle until full darkness, after which time I could be swiftly transferred to a closed litter and taken there where it was commanded that I should be taken.

The day passed swiftly enough. My thoughts were over-full. There was the living image of the scene in the Morning Nile, all blended, somehow, with the captain's words that had also stirred my depths.

My needs were provided for, good food and facilities for the care of my body. But these things I had grown accustomed to. Of the Men of Khem, one could not say that they "lived comfortably," though much later in the history of their land those words would have been an under-statement. But even at this early time, the years of the shaping of Egypt, the reasonable amenities of life were provided for. And as far as I had been able to see such things, such modest care for the things of the body reached down into the ranks even of the hand laborers. To us moderns, the provisions for them would seem scanty. Yet these were simple men, of simple needs. And those needs were more than met. The villages of artisans, for instance, near the building place of a great temple: I remembered reading the shocked reports of modern archaeologists concerning these.

Our Twentieth Century contemporaries visualized them as true "slave camps." I was to learn much of such places in the months just ahead of me. And I, who had always wondered at, for instance, the light-hearted sketches of animals drawn on limestone flakes, for pure pleasure, at those same "slave camps," I found my wonder at our offended scholars' conclusions justified.

These men were *alive*. They were doing, gladly, service to their God-King—for such the Pharaoh appeared to them, and this not, as I was learning, without reason. For their service they were reasonably compensated. And further, the work was done during the Flood Months, the time when the life-giving waters of the Nile were on most of the land. As this had been a farm and gardening civilization, and remained so to a very large extent, *all* business slowed at that time throughout all the land.

With surmises about these things, concerning which I was later to learn much, and meditating on the strangeness of my personal fate, the daylight hours passed quickly enough.

CHAPTER III

I Meet the Golden Horus

After dark, and before the rising of the moon, I heard a soft hail from the shore. Our captain answered. Soon, his footsteps were audible on the deck. Silently he came to the shoreward side of the little cabin. He pulled the draperies apart and motioned me to follow him.

A few feet across the deck and I was ashore, then seated in a covered and closed litter. The bearers made fast time, their walk was half a running.

Soon a voice, low-pitched but peremptory, and unmistakably military, halted us. One who had ridden in a similar litter just behind me—the commander of the little party—stepped out and spoke a few words to the officer of the guard. We moved forward again.

In a little more than a minute after that the motion stopped and my litter was gently let down to the ground. I was directed to step out. The leader of the party took my arm. In the few seconds before we had gone through a narrow doorway I saw that we had stopped in a wide courtyard, lit dimly yet sufficiently so that no one could pass through it unseen.

The room I found myself in, cheerfully bright with the glow of many oil lamps scattered about on low tables, was simply furnished. Yet even by modern standards the simple objects were magnificent. There were dishes of fresh fruit on a table beside a low, backless folding stool. The dishes were of stone, perfectly cut and beautifully polished. The table, of ebony, was inlaid with bands of gold. A bed on the other side of the room, which was about ten yards square from wall to wall, had on it sparkling fresh sheets of that fine linen, some of which had survived (in tombs) to the Twentieth Century, where they could be viewed in our museums.

The man who had brought me, young and personable, and clearly of a high intelligence, had the mark of the courtier upon him. It was subtle, but obvious, showing in a suavity of manner, in a control notable even among a people who prided themselves on, and always made efforts for control. At the same time that I was sensing this I was struck with the complete truthfulness of the portraiture of the statues that had come down to us from this early period.

This young man of the Great King's household had less of the African softness that had been evident even without trace of Negro features, among the family of that nomarch far to the South, with whom I had been dwelling for those first weeks. Here was a stocky fellow, with the planes of his face more square-cut. And while he was darkly-tanned as all the rest, from the Egyptian sun, it seemed to me, at least in the lamplight, that his skin had a more Caucasian paleness.

Later I learned that he was, as I had surmised, of the royal blood, a descendant, along with the King, of those invaders who had come in from the direction of Persia more than a thousand years before.

These, as I was to be told later, had shared the rule of the Valley between them—one branch near the Delta, the other far to the South. The tradition, oral history really, and at this time still alive, had it that these Sons of Horus, united in their Temple Priesthood, where they worked as one, had carried Khem a long way on the road of her evolution. Then, when it seemed to the King of the South, the great Narmer, that Union was called for, his Brother in the North was loath to give up royal perquisites. War had followed, and the smiting of many heads, and over a heap of slain the union had been consummated.

The Prince, despite his—I can only call it—bluff appearance, spoke softly, even gently. He informed me that his brother, the Divine Horus, (he whom we know as Menkare or Mycerinus), was still at the funeral temple of the old King where he was needed for further rites at sunrise the next day. Then he would

21

be returning to the City, for the business of the Kingdom could not wait and there was much awaiting his decision.

He said that ordinarily a stranger in the land might have to wait long before his fate was decided. But my case was—here he allowed himself a little smile—"somewhat unusual." He thought the King would see me soon.

"That you are here, in one of our guest apartments, and not in the prison," he went on, "is something for which you may give thanks to the one that serves my Royal Brother in the South.

"He sent a good report of you, and while the tale is, mortally considered, hardly believable, many strange things are happening at this time all up and down the length of this our Land of Black Earth.

"Be of good cheer, and sleep now. I will see you at the time of the first light, in the hour before the birth of Tomorrow's New Sun."

I soon lay down on the bed, without much expectation of sleeping. Yes, there was so much, there were so many crucial things awaiting me tomorrow. I was sure I would never be able to sleep. But I found, as I had so often during the weeks before this, that there was something about the land of Khem that could quiet even a Twentieth Century Western Man. Not that the people of old Egypt were drowsy. They were gay and lively, and their waking hours filled with activity—each man according to his station but all, judged by modern standards of limited hours of work, endlessly busy. Yet, when the time for resting came, they rested. There was an inner peacefulness "in the air" around these people, a quiet that, I was growing more and more to think, grew in a ground of inner strength. They had a surety we moderns lack. I can only ascribe it to their never feeling alone and comfortless in a harsh world. These men "knew" that the Divine Spiritual was around them, not doing their tasks for them, yet always ready to give the strength needed by a man for carrying his work through.

Be all this as it may (I expect to *convince* no one, I merely report), I was, by a kind of osmosis, acquiring more inner quiet than I ever had known. The fateful interview with the Great

22

King, the chance that by the next nightfall I might have drawn my last breath, adjudged an object of danger to the Kingdom—something which, to me, even then, would have seemed a reasonable judgment in the light of the direction that my continued presence might well give to the whole course of things—none of this disturbed me.

I lay on the bed and adjusted the hard headrest under my skull and was soon in deep sleep. I dreamt, at least I think it was a dream, that three shaven-headed ancients, each carrying an oil lamp of alabaster and dressed in white linen robes, came in softly on sandaled feet and stood for a long time motionless near the foot of my bed, observing me in silence. These then, dream figures or palpable men, left as they had come and the room was dark again, except for one small lamp that a servant had left burning earlier.

Waking very early, I was glad that I could anticipate the Prince. I washed carefully all over me, and put on one of the clean robes that I found among the things in baskets along the farther wall of the well-appointed room. I had eaten of the fruit piled on the table near the two chairs, when the Prince came in again.

The young man—he must have been in his middle twenties—greeted me cheerfully and wished me well. He spoke without condescension and yet not as to an equal, and with it all he put me completely at my ease.

He spoke mostly of his brother, Menkare. It was definite now, he said, that I was to be brought before him before the Sun had come to his full height in the sky.

"I think," he told me with that slightest hint of a smile that I had noted in him before, "that the Divine Horus has still, even since the rites of accession, a full measure of human curiosity. He always has had that.

"His counsellors told him there were many things more pressing, administrative questions, judgments in cases where the litigants had exercised their right of appeal to the King Himself, many diverse matters. As I heard the tale just now, my brother laughed.

" 'I will do my tasks the better after I have satisfied myself at least a little as to this strange, pale man,' he said."

The Prince, who had sat down while he was talking, motioned me (commanded me by gesture would perhaps be a truer word for it), to take the chair on his left. Then he startled me further by laying his hand upon my knee.

"It lies in me, heavy as a doubt yet with the lightness of powerful hope," the Prince went on, "that you, O puzzling stranger in whom we can find nothing that is not of the Truth, though all unbelievable, the hope lives in me that the Gods may give you to understand our King when you are before him. So much depends on this, for where there is not mutual understanding there must be enmity. This is true even for the greatest of the great, though they would deny it as applying to themselves.

"Remember, O tall man who hast learned our speech so well one might almost think you were returning home, remember words can be strong yet in themselves they never take us into the heart of any man. The seeing of hearts requires an inner maturity than can *live within* the being, deep within the essential being of the other one concerned.

"Soon now, for the King's ship is swift, they will come to bring you before him."

He instructed me then in the court procedure, the entry before the throne, lying flat—"that floor is very clean," he said, this time with a smile unmistakable—"lying flat unless otherwise commanded.

"Yet the essence is this, Thou Dweller in the West from far beyond the shores of pyramids and ancient tombs, the essence is: the King's ship brings to his Palace now a man younger in years than you.

"This is a man who just in recent days has had to sacrifice much that is dear to him, his freedom to go up and down in Khem, inspecting, planning, himself developing the engineering works that help the God, Hapi, to bring the blessings of Nile Water to our fields. He has given up his freedom to go up and down Khem consorting, to a degree at least, with the People of Khem.

"That is all past for him now. Our words for Majesty and for Being as a Slave are close related and inscribed with the same sign in the godly writing. He is now limited as a man.

"At the same time—and I speak Truth to you—this Certain One we call Menkare is now in actuality Divine. He is, by sacred rite and by his free, willing acceptance, become a Horus. He is still flesh and blood, with the needs of flesh and blood even in some ways heightened. At the same time he is One with the God, united with Him who is the True Offspring of Osiris.

"So, bear yourself humbly, dear stranger, for I would see more than the shell of you later this day. I speak now of an inner humbleness, for believe me, He will know.

"You must understand that that which is Divine is compelled by its own laws to exact respect for the essence it carries.

"I can say no more. You comprehend me or you do not. Your very life is bound up with these things.

"I go now. Servants will bring meats. Nourish yourself, for you will need strength of body. Be in Peace."

The Prince walked gravely from the room, his head low, as though inspecting the cool marshland scenes outlined in color on the floor tiles of the room.

The meal, mainly a superbly roasted joint of tender veal—again I surprise myself as I write these things down from recollection—I did it full justice and was able to eat with none of that inner constriction of stress that can lead one to wish he had not taken food.

I was still engaged with it when again I heard footsteps. It was the old Court Chamberlain, still a powerful man despite his years, yet grown a little heavy around the middle. I remember that my thoughts were not on the interview ahead of me, rather my thought was: "with food like this over the years, it is no wonder."

His servants, younger men carrying staves, a kind of guard of honor I felt them to be, were ranged behind him. The old man, a great soldier in his day, the Prince had told me, gave me a smile I can only describe as benign. It held the gentleness of true human understanding.

"Be never filled with fear," he said. "Some measure of fearing is good for any man. Yet the will of the Gods of Egypt is a Good Will. Even pain is *their* gift, and is for the enlarging of our hearts. Come in Peace, speak Truth before the King, and there will be gladness for you. This I promise. Our King is just."

The old General made me walk just behind him. The youths with staves were ranged on either side of me. Guards or bailiffs? It did not too much matter.

There was, in actuality, not far to walk. The courtyard was sun-bright. I looked up into the brilliant Egyptian sky. The blazing sun blinded me a little, even in those few seconds. Blinking refreshing, cooling tears, I concentrated on the back of the chamberlain. Soon I was turning, a pace behind him, as we entered a cool passage, relatively the longest part of our processional pathway. Before we got to the end of it, the great Hall of Audience that I could see opening out before me, I was as ready as I was ever going to be.

Brilliance of color was my first impression. Walls and pillars brightly painted were almost painful to the modern eye in their vividness of color. A foil to this was the universal whiteness of the robes, diaphanous in the case of the younger, heavier the more to cover the older, grosser bodies. And on the whiteness was, as contrast, the yellow shining of the Sun Metal, gold. Gifts of the King (in this case, of a new accession, actually the largesse of the King's father), were the great gold collars most of the men wore. The women, in the strands of their black wigs, that were in fact head-dresses, not wigs as the word has meaning for us, wore filigréed jewelry, of gold and bright stones and wonderfully crafted.

What followed happened briefly in time, and was essentially far from "dramatic." That is the difficulty in such a report as this: one is tempted to embellish the story—the reader is prepared for signs and wonders—yet I owe a higher duty to truth than to the entertainment of such readers as this work may have. The experience, all of it through those months, not just the high points, was at all times powerful and impressive. Yet the power in it is hard to suggest in words. Looking back,

I think its impact lay chiefly in the exposure to a people so utterly different in their inwardness from us. They were, from King to deckhand on the Nile ships, a people of a fantastic degree of inner force. This came, I think, from their directness and simplicity, their living heartily in each present moment, uncomplicated by the webs of our abstract intellectuality that enmesh us all, be we of the "intelligentsia" or not.

I went as I had been instructed, walking to the prescribed distance from the Great King, then casting myself flat on the pavement before him—a lovely, ceramic tiled flooring which, I noticed, was clean as a new-washed dining plate. Kissing the ground was no hardship.

There had been no way for me to get an impression of the man seated on the raised throne-chair there above me. My eyes had been correctly cast down. Lése-majesté, I knew, was no light matter in those times. Now I lay with nothing visible to me except a little patch of the bright, cool pavement. I waited for a word or a sign.

A hush, deeper than before, had come over the great hall. Through the silence I heard quick footsteps. Then I saw two feet, clothed in sandals, that were simple though well-made. The figure stooped, strong hands grasped both my shoulders to raise me up.

I came to my feet, my neck still bowed. A gentle voice said:

"Look in the face of Khem, the face of Egypt."

I complied. The statues of Menkare, and several have survived to modern times, are excellent likenesses—as one would have assumed. But stone cannot convey what is soul essence. The features of this King held profound gentleness, born out of compassion. This was unquestionable, for in the lines of the face there was no hint of that other sort of gentleness, also real in its way, that can grow out of simple human weakness. The set of the jaw and the force in the eyes belied any such possibility.

The King—I was reminded of the name of his pyramid, "Menkare is Divine"—looked at me a full minute, at me and through me, seeing deep into my being and seeing past me to

27

the good and ill that I, and I felt, *also the times I had so strangely left*, bore in themselves.

I could note, then, a softening of the impersonal intensity, for my eyes had never left his since that one command. He murmured something without bothering to turn his head. I caught only the word "gold."

One of the Lords behind him came forward with a heavy gold collar, simply wrought but beautiful and, as I knew enough to know, tremendous in its implications. A mark of royal favor familiar enough in later times, and, obviously now, already used as such this early.

The Divine King laid it on my shoulders, and his sad face held a trace of smiling as he spoke to me.

"May you be as a good servant to This Land and to the Gods of This Land, both now and in your later journeyings, O Man of the West."

The spell of silence in the room was broken after the King had said these words to me. And out of the murmur of many voices I could distinguish at least one who said, "That one surely is of the Sea Peoples. Our Lord is wise to put him in his service. Ever are they full of guile. So this one will discover, in his wanderings, that which this land should know."

Then they had me docketed in their minds, these courtiers, as one of the sea rovers from beyond the Mediterranean. That was good. Perhaps, if courts and court circles had always been pretty much the same in their essence, I was even hearing the beginnings of a "planted" story.

The King turned abruptly from me, but not before I had the wit to bow low and murmur humble thanks. I withdrew in the fashion I had been instructed, finding my way somehow back to the great doors. There a white-robed servant stood, bowed when he saw me, and led me back to my own room. Respectfully, he urged me not to leave it.

Later that day the King's younger brother returned. Smiling, he said, "You did well. By your *not* calling attention to yourself through strange or stumbling behavior, you have made yourself to be soon forgotten as but one of the many passing through. Thus we here are left the more free that your time as our guest may be to the greatest good.

"Rest through this day. Tonight the Divine Horus visits you, and for him nights are as days. It would not be well to seem to be weary in his sight."

Through the bright hours of the Egyptian sunlight, only sensed indirectly in that sheltered room, I mostly lay upon my bed and pondered. I still did not see at all clearly the shape of the days before me. But it did seem evident that there would, at least, be no sudden ending of them—they meant me well, the ones who had the determining of events in this river valley.

Food was brought to me: at noon a well-cooked fowl, beets and a boiled green vegetable. In the evening the main dish was a delicately broiled fish, filleted, dressed with a mildly spiced sauce. And the bowl of fruits was kept replenished by the servant who looked in on me at frequent intervals. I said "in the evening." Actually, on that day the evening meal was brought me in the late afternoon with a murmured word that the Lord would surely wish to be in readiness betimes.

I sensed the connection with that of which I had been warned. Eating more hastily than usual, I remember that I was at the same time surprised at a calm that let me still savor the food. It would not be true to say that I felt unconcern at the interview before me. But I was not *concerned*. Certainly I was in the grip of powers beyond any of my own; not only did this have to do with the strangeness of my journey itself, it was rather that the people, and especially the leaders of the people, had a force simply lacking in the modern man. I remembered how, back in that future to which I am now returned, we had, looking at the statues of the Great Kings, wondered how we would behave were one of them suddenly to walk, embodied, into the room where we were.

At that moment the silent hinges of my doorway turned. The paneled door was swung into the hallway and through the opening there strode the Lord of Khem, King of the Land of the Black Earth. I sprang to my feet and started to throw myself in full obeisance down before him.

Here, alone with me in the room—for his servant, who had

again closed the door, remained behind in the passageway—he smiled broadly.

"Not here," he said, "not when we are just two. My times are always short and we have tasks too great for wasting even moments."

I was at a loss for the regulating of my behavior. This King, with his own hands—I had time to notice that they were strong and capable—gathered cushions from the bed, strewed them on the floor before it where the side of the bed would make a back-rest, then sat himself in the chair opposite and waved me to a seat on the pillowed ground in front of him.

"We have had intimations of your coming," said the King.

"Respectfully, I would ask, how could that be?"

"Laws, Divine Law, Maat, all happenings are ruled by it. Our Fathers came out of the East to bring this River Land to know the Light as more than radiance, more truly real than just hot sunlight. So in the Divine Balance it was clear that one had to come from the West, and must come soon. For these are the years of the forming of patterns. When I too become an Osiris, these must have been set, as the clay that can only be worked for so long by the potter lest it develop hidden cracks in drying out, before the baking.

"That one would come from the West, we knew well. That he would be out of the future, as the Sons of Horus marched out of the Ancient Past, is clear enough now that the event is made real. Yet we had not foreseen this as it has happened, for to our knowledge it could not be possible."

"Perhaps," I interjected, "I might be able to make some small return for your gracious kindness. Many men, in all ages, have wished that they could know something of the future."

The King smiled broadly again. "A dream in our day also. And on occasion, as later events have shown, it has been given to men to have such knowledge. Yet if the task and purpose of life is the teaching, the maturing of men through many lives—by way of much pain with a little joy—and the learning of peace through sacrifice. . . ." He paused for a long minute before he went on.

"No, this must be a clever snare arranged by Set himself.

30

Were I to learn what is to be, all that for you *has been,* I would be no more than a blinded slave carrying out commands without the light in my own eyes to show the way. No, I must forbid you to speak, not condemn you to muteness or rip out your tongue but rather lay command upon you that you do not ever speak unasked to me or any man about that which you knew of the Story of Khem before you stepped out on our outpost island in the South."

I nodded, bowing my head, saying, "I have kept such silence until now, not wishing to jeopardize my lot. But how can you forego foreknowledge? I respect the strong man who came to that decision, as well as the majesty of the King."

He looked at me strangely. "How can these be separated, the one from the other? Our hearts, it is clear, view life with different eyes. Yet men tell me that you too are truly a servant of Maat, that your words are true."

"Set," I answered, "has made much progress since your time. Our thinking, our perceiving, has departed greatly from reality, from that which truly *is.* At the same time there are many among us who rebel against that Lord of Lies, the Great Ensnarer. And in essence, though their words would not be these, my journey in time, in a machine of his devising, grew out of the dream and hope that from your World Age I might bring back with me that which can help men re-connect with the Divine and so in consciousness, not avoiding Life, to re-establish in their beings, Peace.

"Your very use of the word 'Hotep,' the same for Peace and for Sacrifice, for inner calm and for the deed of a renouncing, provides, I think, a clue to what I seek."

Here, for the reader, I must interject that I report the thoughts I tried to convey and which Menkare, through an unquestionably tremendous intuition, was able to lay hold of in my stumbling Egyptian speech. The literal words I used would mean little in English. So too, what he said then and later is given, fairly and honestly I believe, in its essence and as he would have spoken had he used our modern language.

"But such a thing as Hotep," the King replied, "how could one make a picture for this word save by showing the Altar of

Sacrifice? Without renunciation there is no peace. And the Gods do not strip us bare. As soon as we give up, not things but the desire for things—the object sacrificed is like the picture for the word, a representation true in magic—our arms are filled to their limits with what the Gods bring to us." He divined my thought that arose at these words and went on in the same breath, saying,

"No, I speak not as the King, well supplied with goods. The least of my peasants would say the same to you. The gifts of the Gods to those who have sacrificed their desires are the same for every man: fulfilment of their needs, and peace, true peace with life. The forms, the picture forms of what the Divine Ones bring will vary for each man with each man's station, yet the essence, and in it is the true substance, the essence is the same."

"It would be good, O King, were I then able to see the Life of Egypt as it is, that I in turn might bring back with me later, living pictures in my heart to put in words to show my people these things, in a form that speaks to them from out its own life."

"That might be done," he answered. "My concern is only that we do not contravene eternal laws by letting the tale of your strange visit here creep into people's consciousness. Were all of this a deed of the good Gods— Yet by its nature, such a thing—it cannot be good. Our task must be to transform Set's work into good for men.

"I would take this whole matter to the Temple of the Sun. There dwells the Great God, and those who serve Him are his living implements. You shall come in my train, O Westerner, at least as far as to the antechamber. The inner place, court of the Altar, is open to the sky although surrounded with firm walls. It has to be protected from the eyes of them that might ray evil, might lay their darkness on it.

"There, if the Sun's Self wills it, I and you shall find how to walk further on this strange road.

"On the next night from now, when darkness falls, we make the journey. Be you ready. Then in the early dawn we greet the new-born Sun. When he goes, greying, through the

Western Gate we will, perhaps, have learned the Will of Highest Heaven.

"The Gods of My Land are wise, and tireless. Yet they are as they are in their very title, the *Gods of My Land*. Only the Sun and Stars and the Earth's Own Self, these and the Lord of the Winds that separates them, only these truly know all of mankind. And of them, the Sun is highest and sees all men, sees also future times in the past's embers.

"Rest well my son."

He left me, this man younger in years than I, yet aged beyond me in an agelessness that left no incongruity in the fatherhood. I was overwhelmed with pride. Had not Pharaoh named me "Son?"

To men of the Twentieth Century that would be meaningless, save perhaps as an indication of royal favor. We today have lost the power of perceiving that men are more, or else less, always, than they seem, that, as in this case, a King could embody fatherhood so powerfully in his being that he *was* father to all those around him. Yet this was so intensely true that at first when he was gone I wept, weeping as I had not done since my childhood. And I had no shame in weeping. Even when the servant came and saw me and withdrew again to come back later with the refreshment he arranged upon my table. These were not tears of weakness, nor yet of joy. Rather, I had been taken hold of by a greatness that held me gently in its arms, a greatness that was not *contained* but rather focussed in that man of high bearing who had so quietly left the room.

The time of Kings was done before our Twentieth Century. Some lingered in the world, and where their work had in it still any reality, the trueness of it lay not in inheritances, tradition or the rituals of anointing, but in their individual dedicating of their selves as servingmen.

"Kingly bearing," "royal favor," such and related words are meaningless to us because we can have no experiences to relate them to. In the room of that bright, new-looking palace (I found out later that Menkare had only recently built it for himself) I had been addressed by, and possessed by, Egypt

33

herself. He had not, then, worn the Ureaus, the serpent head-band found on statues and pictures of the later Kings. Yet he had no need to, for its power was in that which had enthroned itself a while upon the little chair in my white room in the white palace in the White-Walled City Narmer built.

I ate a little of the food that was brought me, the delicate melons were my special joy, and then I slept as I had not slept, in fact, since childhood.

Throughout the next day, a quiet one for me as I saw no one but the servant, I tried to study, to analyze my state of consciousness. I was definitely in no trance-like condition. My consciousness, particularly of external detail, was heightened, sharpened, so that I saw things fully and clearly and in the multitudinous smallness that makes up a greater whole. Yet the wholeness, the pervading, living pattern that *is* the reality of this our earthly work-place, sang before me as I had never known life could do, vibrated as a *hearable* harmony. No, not the "music of the spheres," the Hymn of Earth addressed . . . addressed to . . .?

Then it came clear, and overwhelming, . . . Addressed to the Sun's Self!

I was, in all this meditation, being well prepared for the night's journey and for the next day to come.

CHAPTER IV

The House of the Sun

By ship, with the oarsmen pulling heartily, we made our way along the star-lit River. I had opportunity to see the faces of the men—a fair cross-sampling of those called "the slaves of Pharaoh" by modern writers. While I do not expect to be believed by many, I must testify that these were not slave-countenances but those of men who felt themselves as free men, as men feel who are gladly fulfilling their destinies. Also, it is a fact that the "mood" of a group is always a reality that emanates from it, raying out what can only be called a kind of light, or a darkness. And the "feel" of this ship's company was good.

Parenthetically it must be added that there were, among those I encountered during these weeks and months, also actual slaves —from among prisoners taken in Nubia in the quelling of uprisings, and certain natives of the Valley itself condemned to a lifetime of unpaid servitude for various crimes. The difference in their bearing, the relative hopelessness with which they went through all their days and nights had the value, for me, of providing confirmation, by its contrast, of what I saw and felt that night and later among the Men of Egypt.

We reached the Holy City of the Sun in the late hours of the night. This was the place called On, and Heliopolis by the late-coming Greeks, the place that in the Twentieth Century has only an obelisk of Sesostris—with it not even foundation walls or scattered masonry to show where once the ancient Temple was.

Now the walls were standing high. Square, the construction was, and unadorned by statuary or carvings.

35

As the dawn light increased, I was bidden to walk behind the King as we came closer to the structure. Priests met us, bowing before him, and he, in a plain white garment, bowed to them. In a square-pillared antechamber lit by torches, I had to wait as he went through a door into the great courtyard of the sun altar.

Earlier Menkare had said that I was to speak openly with the priests of On, answering all their questions freely and in keeping with the principle of Maat. It lay in his heart, he had told me, that I would be examined. "And you need have no fear," he had continued, "that any harm can come to My Land from this. These servants of the Great God deal with men always with the view only of fostering that which will bring about the growth of every man to godhood."

I started a little at that, this early god-king speaking so?

"Truly, truly," he continued, "we today find our selfhood in our manyness. With right I might be called the One in whom the Land of Khem says 'I' unto herself. Yet, in the future, as the sun-priests say, fate will bring fearful changes— and you, O Westerner, I suspect, know something of it."

"Yes, something of it, O Servant of the Gods," I answered him. "God-forsaken, the men of my own later time do yet sense the fact that their dead world cannot give answers, that their dead eyes cannot see, their ears not vibrate to the sounds about them."

Now I was left alone by him, with a solemn company seated around me. An old priest nodded gravely, saying,

"So they send a man who is not of their ruling hierarchy. That shows me they are still guided, though unknowing, by the great, unseen powers, rulers of the whirlwind, of the pouring rain, of the snows that clothe the high mountains so great rivers may bring floods."

I know well that I held in check my amazement at his last words. But it was as before it had been with the King. A flicker of a smile was in the wrinkles near this old man's eyes as he spoke then in answer to my inner thought.

"You cannot reconcile this with 'The Nile that rises from the depths of Earth,' as our folk lore has it. How do we know

36

of rains, and the melting snows that feed our River? O child, child of the West, can you not see that the people's tale is another part of the truth? If I put it in the words, 'All that comes down as rain and sinks into the earth comes forth at last into the seas, the great and small seas; whence it is drawn up again as mist that disappears to seeming nothingness till it condenses to fall as rain that feeds again the streams and rivers. . . .'

"I see *that* is familiar to you in its half-reality.

"But we were speaking first of the blind powers behind these deeds! Not only are they the Earth's nourishers. They feed and restore life in that in man which his man-living (in thought and word) destroys. The *Great Powers* that indwell the earthly powers sustain all life, and will do so, as long as life is still embodied here on earth.

"Yet These alone, They would lead man to destruction, would toss him as a river ship would be tossed and die on the great Western Deep.

"The Guides—and they must still be functioning in your dead world or you could not have lived to come to us—the Guides and Guardians are Heaven's Seed. These are the littlest children of the Sun, and serve our Sun Lord as they tend His flocks.

"What know you of the Sun Lord, sheep of the West?

"To guide you in the shaping of your answering, I must say to you:

"We know:

"That in our World Age He is on His way to Earth; that He will pass the portal of man-birth, be slain, arise, depart and yet remain."

I knelt, in tears, before that old man then. But he, laughing, raised me and said,

"It is not my virtue that I know these things. Our priest-kings, the hidden scrolls will tell you, learned all of this, and more, with things that have to do with times as far from your times as yours from ours, out of the Book of Thoth before it was cast down into the waters.

"What we pour into Khem is only the food Her children

need. The rest is stored away in all the great, unembodied temples. . . .

"Lost in your time, you are thinking:

"I say to you, these things can never be lost. It is not in the nature of their Being that men could lose them."

"Yet, the Sun God came, and died," I answered then, "and men have lost Him in my age, have been given a shadow form of a Great Preacher standing before the people, mouthing honeyed rules of conduct.

"The God who died that men might live, and work with Him creating the New Earth and the New Heavens—He is lost!"

The old Sun Priest's next words, in answer to this cry of mine, were gently spoken, and yet were like great peals of thunder and rolling blasts:

"No God, even the least God of a village well, is ever lost.

"He may withdraw an hour, or for a thousand years. Yet that too, when it happens, is His deed, because men have need of such withdrawal, never can it be called 'their Losing of him.'

"In their time, will all the Company of the Gods again be on the march, and go in the sight of men. And in that marching, man and every represser of mankind will have his rightful place, for Maat Herself will guide him to it."

"You call those Powers 'blind' to which, in my earth age men give themselves," I ventured, questioningly.

"The men of every age of human growth," he answered, "walk in full blindness over against that of which their *seeing* would confuse them. And the same holds true, always in its degree, for Spirit Powers—be they above man or beneath him in their own right stage of growth.

"Even the mighty, the primeval Powers that are the helpers of the great Earth Being—These that bring seeding, growth and death in season—These dare not be distracted from their deeds. Were They to sense the passions that tear the soul garments of *one man*, of even one earth man, They could be rendered impotent with terror.

"So the high and holy Ones, the Lords that serve the great

38

Sun's Self, pour blindness on their offspring, the Powers of Growth that labor in the Earth.

"Thus These can continue mightily to labor that Earth may bring forth all her fruits in season and properly draw her breath that is, for me, the solar year. And Man, who is to be that to which Earth, saying "I," can point, this human child is still nourished, and must be for ages yet, at the deep breasts of the full-bodied mother.

"Her milk would cease to flow were she concerned with guiding him among the crocodiles along the shores where he must go.

"Man soon will waken inwardly again—I speak of your time—and learn to call upon other Gods, Who open up the Way.

"He will find the Sun Lord then, never to be, himself, thus lost again. . . ."

Simultaneously with these last words there came an earthquake shock, not heavy but unmistakable, and premonitory. I had been carried, by what he said, to heights. I was jolted back to my body and, incidentally, to my Twentieth Century consciousness. Though in a sense I knew better from what I had already learned within this time and place, I must confess I now expected to see Ancient Man, overawed by fearful powers, cast himself down and cry aloud for help. At the same time I was wishing I could get out from between these stone walls.

By now they were trembling again. All this, of course, took less time than the writing or the reading of it needs.

The priest's voice *was* raised:

"Out from here, and quickly. To the open space of processions, beyond the outer pylons. Let the three youngest, running, make search of all the rooms, and chambers of meditation, and clear them likewise—by my command. We go."

The most aged and weak as to body were assisted in making haste. With no other voice heard in our company, an efficient evacuation of our room was carried out.

In the midst of the wide area before the temple we were joined by others from the building, last of all by the three youngest, who bowed before that Chief of Prophets, as the

39

High Priest of On was then already called, and reported that there were none unaccounted for.

"What of the King?", I asked him, for I knew that the court of the high altar was well shielded within the walls.

He smiled gently and told me that the place where Menkare then was was far enough from its screening so that even if the walls did topple, not even flying stones could do him any injury.

"Yet, I do not think that this will be a severe one. It did not give that feeling.

"Nevertheless we must stay here an hour. We know this is a slipping of the outer crust of the earth, and when the tensions are not fully adjusted, there can well be more trembling."

Try as I might to imitate their own outward impassivity, things still always showed through, especially when I was startled, as now, to hear what might have come from an educated "modern man."

"The Wise have *always* known these things," he said, voicing it in such a way that my pride stayed untouched. "Surely you see that the people at large cannot grasp them. How many can in your time, I wonder. Such knowledge stems chiefly from accurate observing, swayed not by feelings."

He waited, patiently, for some reply from me.

"I would have thought," I replied, "I would hear you say 'The Nether Gods are angry.' "

This time he smiled.

"And perhaps they are," he replied. "One could see reason for their anger in your presence here, upsetting the inner balance of the circling flow of time. Yet we know that on earth the Divine (self-existent even without the earth) expresses itself always through earthly instruments."

In due time, he nodded at his helpers and we rose and returned to the inner council hall, where he taught us further as though nothing had occurred. And Menkare, on his return and later, made no reference to the earth shock, which he too must have felt. Suddenly now the priest interrupted himself in the midst of a phrase:

40

"But to our present task. The young King returns from the High Altar with a full heart.

"Down on your faces, all," he spoke in sharp command, himself dropping flat on the chamber floor.

We lay facing the doorway through which the King had left us. I dared not to raise my head, yet I was conscious, somewhat as a sleeper is, of a Presence there above me where I lay, my forehead pressed to the cool tiling. Tenderness as I had felt it in his Hall of Audience, gentleness of feeling flowed from what was centered in that human body. His word to us was to rise from the ground. Then he spoke further as though I were not present:

"Men of Egypt, who are to me as devoted fellow-servants, the Great God has said to me,

" 'Let it be as though this light-haired stranger had less being than a dream you have had on waking from deep sleep. Yet if any would, within your Household, come near to him, allow them. There will be no evil come of these things, although seeming evil for a little moment. For whatever arises, let no one be punished.

" 'There is but one command : He shall not be outside your kingly household and my household here in this my temple. Were it otherwise, men would be frightened, and given still more than now to losing their way.'

"So the God spoke. If any here would question the man who tells this speech, he is commanded to let his words be heard.

"It seems to me that this man comes to us partially conscious at the least, of what he has to do.

"We dare not interfere with what the work of Set, against the Powers of Heaven—I speak of the Time Ship—has been destined by the Great Gods to be.

"We can only be as servants, seeing as far as it is given us to see, conscious, and beholden to the Great God, within the limits of our seeing. . . ."

To me these last words made a balance for the old priest's earlier picturing of Nature's blindness. Now he spoke again.

"Maat rules," and these words seemed addressed to me rather than to the King.

"Maat rules," that priest repeated then. "We may have trust in the Sun's Messenger, whether this be our King or yet it be the Lady Maat herself who speak through him. The Child of the West shall be welcome in the Great House of the Sun as in the Great House of the Lord of Egypt. Let him walk in both houses as the child of both their Lords.

"Another word is born in me: that help can come to far, far distant earth-men.

"O Majesty of Egypt, be his task while he is here, to learn the teachings given us in past ages, to learn them so that he cannot forget them. In your own house let him be in the company of your small children. From the aged and the babes he shall learn to know this people. Then, in his future he shall do what the Gods command him to do."

CHAPTER V

The King's Daughter

With little ceremony there ended thus my first visit to the lost Shrine of On, the place of which the later Greeks would speak as the Sun City. Back in the great capital of the White Wall, I became part of the household of the King. And when I learned to know the men who taught the sons of his Queen, men wise in their apparent simplicity, I blessed the name of the High Priest of On. Yet as I did so it was as if I heard his voice, "The teachers, yes, but the child is wiser still. Study the child, O thou who truly willest to mature. He will teach thee adulthood."

I was three weeks among the princes, I grey-headed, studying with them the tasks their teachers set them, before I met the Great King's daughter. She was a girl of seventeen, and when I saw her I marveled. She was not like any of the representations left us from that Old Kingdom time, not earthy and deep-bosomed, but delicately beautiful as were those royal ladies that later bore the Amen-Hoteps in the time of Egypt's third great blossoming.

I gasped when I first saw her. She, with the disconcerting ability they all possessed, read my thoughts and smiled as she came in through the doorway of my room, where I had again been eating.

After stopping the obeisance I would have made, saying, "I am not truly royal. In this too is the reason that you wonder at the way I am made in this, my body.

"My mother was not of the blood that rules here, nor even a child of any of the King's Companions. She was of the early people of this Valley, dark and slight. He, Prince of Egypt, saw her when he was out fowling in the Delta marshlands. He never thought to see her again, and never did. Yet as his girl-child grew, there were those who thought she was beautiful. But the servants of the Royal House said, "Wait, this belongs to the Prince, it is his, let us at least show him his own.

"I was brought here discreetly, and the One who now reigns in Khem said, 'Let her be as are my other daughters.' "

All the time that she was speaking she was moving gracefully about the room, straightening my rumpled bed, taking used dishes out into the hallway, then bringing one of the little folding chairs so like our "modern" ones, and setting it across from me at the little table that held garden fruits, grapes and golden melon slices.

Daintily, she herself began eating. Perhaps understandably, I was at a loss for words. Smiling again, she said,

"Speak what is in your heart, have no fear. You too are of this household. My Royal Father told us."

"You," I said, stammering, "were doing as a servant. . . .

"Yet any of my *royal* sisters too, would, were there no servant near. So are we taught to do. The Princes go out in the quarries to learn how good building stones are found and shaped. And there lend their hands to a struggling quarry crew, they. . . ."

Involuntarily, I interrupted, "But none of this is what the later world will know of Egypt."

"Because," she answered, "the little they will know will be of a far later Egypt, old and pompous."

While she was speaking I remembered that our archaeologists had learned (from laundry marks on linen, and tomb inscriptions) how in one of the early dynasties the royal launderer was one of the King's own intimate nobles. I nodded silently at her.

Without any of that which later ages would call wantonness she reached her delicate hand across the table and touched my cheek.

"But still you are wondering," she said. "You have no need of shyness."

Looking full at her, I stammered,

44

"I wonder that you are here, alone with me. Your Royal Father said. . . ."

"My Royal Father," she interrupted me, her dark eyes sparkling from within their circles of the green eye shadow that looks so strange to us in their paintings yet in life was fitting to these ladies, "My Royal Father knows that I am here. I told him I was curious about you. He looked all through me, and it was as if the Uraeus, seldom used, were gleaming on his forehead. Then he said, almost solemnly,

" 'Go in to him. This too has been foretold. As man I do not understand it, yet as Egypt—in these weeks a man has become a people—as Egypt I am conscious that this must be. Let no one be punished, so ran the words.'

"Then he smiled at me, with that divine tenderness that makes us all adore him, and turned back to his work. He was deciphering an ancient leaden tablet, dictating words to his scribe. The Prince Herutataf stood near him, full of eagerness.

" 'You did well to bring me this,' I heard the Father saying as I left his chamber. 'It must be put with the other writings that we gather. Buried, you say you found it, in the earth before the feet of the God's Statue?' "

She left the subject, and her eyes shone with mischief.

"So here I am, with you. Is your heart not glad?"

Her hand rested lightly over where my heart was.

"O Great Lady who reads my thinking," I said, managing a smile along with my trembling, "surely your fingers feel the not-so-distant drumming there beneath them. Need you ask? But I would ask you one thing, what is the name you carry?"

"He," she answered, "gave me the name of Nutka, the Ka or Double of the Heavenly Mother who is the Lady of the Starry Sky. I remember the time well. He had been gazing at me in silence and then he said,

" 'We called each other Geb and Nut that night among the reeds. She said I must be the Earth Father Himself. I told her she was surely Nut embodied. And this little one grows to be like her. Let her be called the Ka of her mother, Nut.' "

I sat looking at her, saying nothing. She was quiet, in that complete bodily repose that reflects in their statues we moderns know. In all those people it was something effortless, growing out of an inner calm and sureness. Yet for her, at that moment. . . . One might have thought she was at some temple service.

Only one thing betrayed her, the sparkle, as of a child in mischief, that remained in her deep, great eyes. Finally she spoke again, since I still said nothing:

"You wonder at me, that a mere curiosity, a woman's whim, should bring me here beside your bed.

"O stranger, those were *words* I gave you first. Yet they were far from lies. Maat is my witness, I *am* curious about you. My Father-King will tell me nothing when I ask him. But I have been watching you since first you came here, do not ask me how. And you are become lovable. Gentleness, kindliness, and in a great Lord such as you are. Respect towards the least of those who wait upon you, as though they were true men rather than slaves. None of our nobles here, none even of my brothers are like you. Only the One who has become the King, the new Golden Horus, my Father, he is more like you than you are to yourself. He is kind and gentle and already there are those who murmur that Egypt will suffer, having now a King who is not like the noonday sun, slaying by his fire those he looks too long upon. What makes you like to him?"

"In times to come there will be many legends about your Royal Father," I said to Nutka. "His name will truly live forever, even though the stories will be garbled and untrue. Long after *this* present time there will come a Greek traveler gathering these tales, and in them, those who are wise will read the heart of a good man and truly noble King."

Now the balanced quiet of her lovely face was shattered. She looked at me in wonder, and in the wonder I saw even a little fear.

"How come you to speak so—about that which is to be?"

I had been thinking aloud and had not given thought to how my words would seem to her who sat before me. Now, unwittingly, I had broken the King's command. Yet I could not leave her in that mood of questioning. She would only turn to others, and matters would be even worse.

"Will you swear," I asked her, "give your word, by Maat and in the sight of all the Gods of Egypt, to speak to no one of these things, unless your King should ask you? Answer him fully and completely, for I would rather be put to death than urge you to untruth."

She looked now like a very little child. Her words came in a soft murmur.

"Breaking that word would condemn me in the Judgment of Osiris. I would have to die the Second Death."

"I know it," I answered her, equally solemn.

"In the name of Maat Herself, the Sun-born messenger of Truth, I swear what you would have me swear—Silence, save only if Menkare ask me," she said then, in a voice grown firm again.

So I told her of how I had come to be in this palace, omitting nothing relevant. All this, she truly comprehended.

At the end of my telling she drew in deep, long breaths. These were slow and tranquil, her lovely little breasts rising and falling like moon-boats on a gently rolling sea. With each breath she grew stronger, older, rose again from childhood before my eyes.

Silently she sat then, watching me awhile. I was calm also and able to smile at her. Though it seems, perhaps, fantastic in the telling, I knew then what I had suspected before. I knew I loved this girl, younger than I in years, yet older by millennia. It was not just an echo of that first flash of mortal desiring as it had leaped up in me when first I saw her. Bodily love was in it, yet this was a transcendent thing. Nutka was, in her whole being, the Egypt I had loved since I was a boy in the Nineteen Hundreds and had haunted the museums when I was supposed to be out playing in the streets of that city of the West.

She was smiling now, and as a gentle, loving mother might smile at an impetuous boy child.

"So to you I am as the whole Land of Khem, the Egypt you have always loved. That is good, for I will not let you forget that I am Nutka too—this I will see to.

"You wonder, at the same time, at my sure acceptance of

47

this so strange tale that you had to tell me. I who do not know even the name you carry."

"I was called Joseph by my parents, after another who is to visit this, your land, more than two thousand years from now," I told her, interrupting.

She nodded, earnest again.

"This is all according to Maat. O Joseph, you are beautiful to me—yet this alone would never bring me here." Her hand embraced the room in a wide gesture.

"A Sun Priest warned me, seven years ago, that I was born for a strange task, a labor I would understand when it approached me.

" 'Nut, whose name you carry,' said the Ancient, 'bears within her body fields of glittering stars. Yet each of these stars, in themselves, is a home of spirit beings, and of these is Sothis the greatest. For from that star came the soul of Egypt, Isis, Astet, who is the eternal starry wisdom and the bride of Osiris, the King of the Blessed Dead.

" 'One day she will enter in you as the cord that binds two ships called Past and Future when they meet awhile in Khem. Be Isis then, and fearless, as long as she is with you.'

"I could never understand this until you came. Yet when I first saw you in the Great Hall, I knew—unknowing still your origin, I knew!

"O My Beloved."

Childlike in the suddenness of her change from these serious words, she stood up, laughing, and slipped her garment from her. I grey-haired traveler in space and time, was young as she was. We had joy together.

When the coldness of the Egyptian night woke me, many hours later, she had gone.

It was three days before I even saw Nutka again. I was walking across a courtyard with two of the young princes and their teacher. We had been studying the elements of their mathematics together. The children, ten and twelve, were tired and, for Egyptian royalty, almost fretful. I was absorbed in watching them and even more in the tutor, a deeply tanned young noble who was back from a year in the rock quarries.

48

"Children of the Horus," he said, unsmiling, "you will be miserable servants to your King if you would not learn how to reckon measurements exactly. He is the First Slave of his people, giving up part of his being that he may serve us. If we will not in our own selves be as servants, the Land of Khem cannot keep us."

"I will go alone across the Desert," said the younger of the boys, interrupting. "I will go far away."

A light footfall behind me made me turn. It was Nutka and she looked past me at the boys as though I actually were the wraith that in essential fact I was as far as all these people were concerned. Inwardly I started to greet her, for I had felt alone through these last days, I to whom the word loneliness had formerly had no meaning. But the lessons Khem had taught me had at least made me so that I could keep my face in repose, and I in no way betrayed the fact that we were not strangers.

Later that night. Nutka confirmed this for me.

"You were as the People of Khem," she said, "outwardly showing nothing of the storms within your being." And she explained to me that although, as I knew, their customs of life were different from ours—different mostly in their frank acknowledgement of that which modern man would hide—there was a decorum in the Palace. "None knows save the One," she whispered, "and it is better that they should not know."

All this was after we had had again our joy in one another.

"You are a strange Joseph," she said. "It is almost as though you had felt gladness as something shameful."

"So, in a sense, we are taught to feel it," I answered slowly, groping for my words. "I believe too that that is necessary, in my world age. For we would quickly become ruthless animals, were such restraints not on us.

"Men have proven this in places where they set out to deny the Great God his worship. For soon the rulers established elaborate codes of that which they called 'public morality.' What men did as to abiding by them may be another story, yet it was deeply felt that. . . ."

"Joseph, Joseph, I do not understand you. Why should men

49

try to deny Heaven its due? And why should priests, or priest-less Kings (another picture I cannot make real), try to tell men that what is natural and glad, is evil?"

"Perhaps because with us such things are unconnected with man's inner being," I replied.

"Yet here, and now, in Khem, in this very moment, these things are also not of our inner being. Put out of our way, as they are for this hour, as we have just made them—now we can truly approach, as we could not before, each the inner self of the Beloved."

"Darling Nutka, for you, for all the Khemti and thus for me as I dwell among you, there is a need—mankind being still young—to come down into the body; and such joys help bring us there. Mankind is still young. . . . No, do not interrupt again, I know your history is already long, I know that more than a thousand years before this your people devised the calendar which, only somewhat changed, men still use in my late time. I know men have walked long, in all these lands. Yet you have not lost *youth*. You still trail Heaven's glory where you move.

"We, even in our youth, are aged, dry. If we grow into too deep an interest in our body, it becomes, for us, an elaborate toy. And grown men should not go on playing with children's toys.

"We have known now, taught by the Sun's Own Self almost two thousand years ago, that the greatest love a man can bear his friend lies in a willingness freely to die if that can succour or guard him."

"The Gods tell you that?", she asked.

"The Great God showed us that," I answered, "and since that hour we are left godless, alone on the earth.

"How horrible."

"Yes, it is horrible. Yet in my deepest self there stirs to life a thought that must have been there a long time, sleeping:

"The Earth could never have continued turning, the Sun would have burned black, without the Gods, the Ones that Western Men call the One God's Servants—Angels, Archangels, Powers and Dominions. O yes, Child of the Dawn, my brothers

50

of the West still speak of the Gods, of the Beings of Power, although by other names.

"Yet what I said a moment ago is no lie. Men have, in my time, actually lost them. They know them just by faith, and their faith is weak, and by memory of what their forefathers wrote in Holy Writings. But this is not the thought that I would tell you.

"My thought is, rather, that the darkest time is over."

Speaking so, filled with these things, I had not noticed Nutka. A resonant voice yet most feminine, hers and yet not her voice, called me now to her. I looked up.

She stood, proud, before me. Her eyes shone in the light of the little lamp that was at the moment the only illumination. Her eyes shone, and without the strange glow that I had, in my modern life, come to associate with mediumism. These were fully conscious, highly wakeful eyes. Her slight, small body stood in straightness and at the same time in full repose. That human garment I had come to cherish in our few, brief hours of nearness, seemed taller, greater than its measurements. I am conscious of how strange it must sound to those who read this, yet in the name of Truth I must write it so. She seemed divine. She had called my name three times, and now she spoke:

"The Cosmic Sunlight that created the eye, must open it again. The Word that echoed first across the endless pasturelands of Heaven to bring this earth to being, that same Word must pour like rain into men's deadened ears, that they again shall hear the Music of Eternity.

"And the Word and the Light shall be accompanied by us. They, Word and Light, the deeds of the Great God, shall be accompanied across the bridges of the sky whose paving is a road that men call Time, shall be accompanied by us who are the Least of all His Servants.

"We, called in Khem the Company of the Gods, the Phut Neteru, We are on the march. We shall be known by other names, or no names. That harms us not; our names are known to Him.

"Another three times seven hundred years shall We guide the Men of Egypt. That is, for us, as less than a day's labors.

And then we start on the long day's journey across the Bridges of the Sky.

"Look well upon me, O Man of the West, forerunner of that Joseph who shall come in our twilight here and whose People shall take gifts of the Holy Wisdom with them. Look well upon me, Joseph Aramath. Few mortals have seen me unveiled."

When she first called my name I had risen to a sitting posture. To stand would have seemed presumption, for I believe that in body I still was taller than she. And I could not bring myself to kneel in front of her, still my Beloved while at the same time she was as a star in the night sky.

This was a woman and yet—I recalled an ancient expression, "filled with the God." In my dry, modern mind it had always brought a picture of bacchantes, drunken with the sacred wine imbibed from clay cups. Now I saw it meant, literally, what it said. This was a God, was even the great Isis, standing before me and claiming no more than angelic rank.

A power in me, perhaps it was simply my true, Eternal Ego, took hold of me then and I did at last sink to my knees in reverent adoration.

"Let there ring forth across the Fields of Peace, Child of the Western Desert-land of Souls," She who stood there addressed me, "Let there resound to meet us, echoing, when we there stand in your parched land, one word of the Ancient Speech—

"Hotep, Hotep, Hotep. And this shall be enough. If god-forsaken men can, in your future, find again, the meaning of *this one word*, then there is hope.

"Hotep. In the holy writing that my brother-husband, Asr, The Osiris, taught to me in the first days there stood this picture of an altar with the sacrifice, the first-fruits of the fields, lying upon it. Hotep, one image-picture word, the same for Sacrifice and for the only Peace mankind can find upon this earth.

"If men in your desert-age can find this living word of Peace again, then we, the Servant-Children of the Sun God shall be able to help them find their Selves again. And finding selfhood they shall find, in their Freedom, the Sun's True Self who walks, unseen, among them. Even now He, the Great God, Son of the Great God, makes His way down from the far Eternal Lands. He goes, to stay, a God, in a human body, to sacrifice Himself to earthly death that they, in Him, might live.

"O wonder not, man-child. His deed and death have been fore-known in Heaven for longer than your very dreams could encompass. Even his trusted servants among the men of earth have long known well of all that is to be. Let men in your own time begin again to know the Laws of Maat, of the Eternal, Cosmic Truths. Then they shall begin to come to the True Freedom, born of Love—of which I am a servant-bearer—and set forth in deed through Hotep, Hotep, Hotep."

That word, three times repeated, echoed as from nearby and then farther and farther away. The Glorious One before me—her eyes were still alight and looking into them I saw, and literally saw, the great fields of the stars.

I turned as a man's voice, low yet resonant, called out behind me:

"My Divine Mother, Holy Wisdom, in my earthly daughter's shape."

Behind where I was, near the doorway, lying prone upon the tiling as his own slaves and servants lay before him as King enthroned, was the Great King, Menkare.

Then, as from a distant mountain came that voice, for the last time, still speaking through the lips of her, his child.

"Your task, for the Children of Khem and thus for mankind, is well known to you, beloved servant of the Servers of the Sun. Where no further word is needed there can be none."

CHAPTER VI

Isis

Now, without any transition, his girl-child stood, with downcast head, before us.

"Dear Father, who has become the Golden Horus of this Land, here is a chair for you to sit."

She took him, as a little child might, by the hand, raised him to his feet and led him over to the simple bedside seat. Herself she seated at his feet and there I joined her.

We were silent a long time. Finally the dam broke in me and I dared to be the first to speak. I voiced the question of a modern man.

"Tell me, Nutka, do you remember any of the words spoken in this room just now? Divine words surely."

She smiled again now, but her eyes were sad.

"How men, even good men beloved of the Gods, do change in all their knowing and not-knowing, down through the ages," she said. "Surely I remember, I know every word I uttered."

"But surely it was the Goddess. . . ."

"Truly, yes, it was the Goddess, yet it was She in me who am the woman-servant of her Heaven-Sister Nut."

"In time to come," I could not help rejoining, "your priests will dream that they, themselves, are gods. I know such thoughts are far from you, yet I could not help imagining you spoke in a kind of waking sleep, where your true self was far away from here."

"The true self of an earth-man is far stronger in the nearness of the Company of Heaven," Nutka said, and she was silent.

"You spoke of a time to come, in this my land. How far

off a time?", the King's first words since he had hailed the Divine Speaker were spoken to me softly.

"Two thousand years, Menkare. And even then, though her life-essences will have left her, Egypt does not pass away."

"In the very old age of a man," he replied, "reality and dream and wish flow all together till he knows not what is his illusion. So it surely can be with a people and their priesthood, living on too long.

"O I have seen it, very near to me. Old age, in an old body, is a curse reserved for those the Gods could teach the truth, could bring to Maat in no other way than by feeding them with untruth as one might fill a drunken fool with too much wine in the hope that his sick head in the morning would show him the final ending of his road.

"Yet that is one punishment they spare me. Seven years, the Chief of Prophets told me. Only seven years are given me to strive to bring my children—all the Khemti are my children —that which they need. The harshness of the Horuses that reigned before me. . . ."

He shrugged, and smiled a sad smile. "Yes, I know that it was needed. First, the Power of Willing; men can learn it only through deeds. And men, as they are today, can come to deeds only through power imposed upon them from above. Then came Thinking—first Khufu, then Chephren, Man of Will, Man of Thought, fierce will, harsh thought."

Like a whiplash came his next words, directly at me.

"What, think you, is the task, then, of Menkare?"

I held my ground, as one who stands against a high wind, and answered quietly:

"The memory of mankind, O Menkare, preserves it to the end of time. It is even in the writings, for those who can winnow Maat from all the dross of garbled tales men tell to travelers from other lands.

"Yours, Menkare, Ego Man for your whole land in an age when the Ego is not yet born among the people, yours it is surely to give them that without which man is only partly man. You embody human *feeling*, true compassion, gentleness. Because the Gods live in the Pharaoh and bring him that which

55

in the later ages men can win by their own living. Thus your House of Eternity, your Pyramid, inverted picture of the pyramid of light that flows from the four directions, is well named. Truly 'Menkare is Divine.' "

"Yet always, always human, and frail human," came the soft voice of power, barely audible. "So much do I wish that I could have you travel with me, up and down this Valley. I would show you, who are my very Son, all that I strive to do in these few years.

"These people need to know their Earthly Father loves them with a true love, yes even when he must slay men for the crimes they do. For the Aton himself rays out love. We, His First Servants, know these things, yet are forbidden to make them known, for men must grow through pain and find each other through feeling they are forsaken. And some even, who have sat in this my seat of power have murmured at this truth and refused it in their hearts. They said, 'Sometimes the priests think the Gods are speaking, when the truth is they are but old men dreaming old men's dreams.'

"But you, my two dear children." He gathered us in his great arms. "Yes, I know well you are become my son through knowing her who is of the royal blood. . . .'"

I looked at him in amazement. We had been secret, and Nutka had told me that servants never came near these rooms except at appointed hours. Were there, then, royal spies, reporting?

He read my thought, and shook his head.

"He who is made King of Egypt gives up much," Menkare said. "Yet, for the sake of his task, for his people, there is that which is given the Kingship in return."

He pointed to his forehead.

"The twin uraei serve me, if I wear their sign or not. In their seeing, I see, and they can see afar. That which concerns my House or has to do with the fate of Khem, I know as it takes place. But fear me not. The body, in my time, is an instrument of learning—though I gather from you that in the later ages, when men are meant increasingly to use it as an implement of work they will wish, as children do, to keep it as among their toys. Yet these are things we both know.

"You, Joseph, have a task for those at the far approaches of the bridge of time. Yours, if you do not fail, it is to bring them the ripe fruits of ancient Khem. What they will do with these, it is not given me to know. Nor need that be your concern if you abide as a servant of the Spirit.

"For you, my Nutka, I feel a father's pain. The laws of Maat, that by which the Gods live, prevent this, your brother's giving anything to us. For we must learn through error and through grief, so that as a race we may grow a little wiser as we age. All memory of him, even among those with whom he holds converse, will fade into an unremembered dream of deepest sleep.

"You, my daughter, also will forget him. This I know. In you will only be an emptiness that you strive in vain to fill. It is not even given me to say if you will be remembered or your name live in my land."

I remembered then the Herodotus legend of the daughter of Menkare, forced into prostitution to help pay for her father's pyramid tomb. I looked at the King. His eyes met mine with compassion, for he knew I truly loved her and felt my helplessness against what I had given her as fate. Yet he smiled as he turned from me to look lovingly again at her, the King's Daughter.

"Yet in the distant ages, child of my body, your name will come forth by day from the tomb where it rested. There will be some, at least, who remember you with gratitude and love. Thus your Ka will be well nourished and appear in a new form.

"Stand before me now, together, for to the eyes of Them, the Twin Goddesses that are my seeing, you are true husband and wife and true children of Khem."

While he was speaking Nutka, on my left, reached her arm around me and rested her hand on my right side. We stood in the position I had seen so often, of the statues of couples, so found in the innumerable tombs. Yet what amazed me was the strength and comfort, a sexless power, that flowed from her right hand. So I was past amazement when I felt, all invisible, on my left side, pulsing with equal power, another hand. He who sat spoke, solemnly.

"There is another, O my son, who stands upon your right and who must stay invisible to you. The Bearer of Isis is known to you, wearing a body of earth-stuff. Yet there must always be, with her, the Other Isis, Nepthys, Nebtet, the Lady of the Temple.

"Isis brings you Cosmic Wisdom, condensed light of the Spiritual Sun. Nebtet, whom you do not see, carries warmth as power, that Will may grow in men and flow to earth as human deeds.

"The whole Book of the Coming Forth By Day, the making all ready of which, still in secret, for the time when men's inner seeing shall grow dim, this is my greatest task. The whole of it can, without lie, be expressed in the words 'Thou hast given me Isis and Nepthys to stabilize me.'

"Man is a Child of Feeling, set in this world to learn, mostly through pain. But the Grace of High Heaven presents him with power for understanding and for turning what he knows to transformation of his planet. Thus and thus only is the senser of earth-things set upright and stabilized. The dead Osiris in his coffin-tree, raised ever again by the Goddesses, is truly stabilized. And with the firmness *given* him becomes a living man.

"In your own age you, Child of the West where Osiris rules, hidden Deputy of the High Sun God, man will have in himself, to carry the Power of Willing. The Deed of Heaven on the mid-point of the Bridge of Time shall have made this possible. Yet he shall still be attended by Cosmic Thought and Cosmic Will, by both these Goddesses. And a Third, my vision tells me, shall be as near to him as these. She is called Cosmic Love, Divine Love, brought to earth by that same deed."

As he paused, meditating, and then turned his face to me, I dared speak again.

"Though the brothers of my World Age only half believe in them, they remember a tradition of such beings and use their names, though only half in earnest. Men call them Angeloi, that means The Messengers, the Messengers of Heaven."

"That is a good name," he answered, "yet what is needful is that all these truths, and all the Laws of Heaven somehow *live* in men again."

"Surely, Great King," I replied then, "there are many Gates to the Land of Truth men call Eternal Life. And He, the God whose Deed you cited, He makes them all stand open. Even in my time men find the pathways to the Gates again.

"If I can bring back with me from this journey, the Spirit Image of One Ancient Gate among the many, the Way of Egypt—Peace through Sacrifice—my task, I think, is carried out."

Menkare was now for a long time silent. And this silence I knew I should not shatter. Nutka and I stood close, before the Initiate. We were content, and somehow, along with the realization of destiny, we were like children, happy in our nearness to each other, needing nothing.

After a time that I could not have measured, because it seemed both short and very long, he rose to his feet.

"Come, O My Son, tomorrow, to my private chamber. The Divine Prince, Herutataf, brings me that which I need to see and touch with my own hands. There is a power in the so-called inanimate, the power of the Spirit as shaped substance took it up. I know, for it is given me to know already, what I shall find written there. Yet I must, in touching it, perceive what the true Ancients, the first Sons of Horus, felt when they made the writing. But enough, you will know of it then."

He left us without further word. We found one another's arms and contented each other. If afterward it seemed strange to me that we could pass so from the Cosmic and Divine to earthly love, I only know that it was not strange then. It was not that our destiny, with the separation coming all too soon, was laid aside. We were clearly conscious of it. Yet the present was all the more real.

We spoke, after a time, of how love can never die.

"If you seek me, My True Brother—for you at least will always remember me—look out in the Starry Heavens. I shall be there, among the stars, serving my Mother Nut, the True

Lady of Heaven, carrier of the Sun that is hidden by night in her great, holy womb."

Then we kissed one another as children might, bidding each other good night. So we slept in peace til the first light of the new day.

Then she went from me, running lightly in her sandals as a little girl might, going swiftly on glad feet. All she said was, "There are some things not for women, since men who are in their eyes often as little children, yet have powers that we lack. We do not complain, to us is given the giving of that without which all their deeds would never be."

CHAPTER VII

The Wisdom and the Three Great Pyramids

I too moved swiftly as the light grew stronger, crossing the courtyard to the King's own doorway. These among whom I was had the force of a pioneer people, these Rulers of Egypt. Racially vigorous they were at this time, and most were individually energetic, early-rising and hard-working all through the hours of daylight. I knew the King's "tomorrow" meant the *beginning* of that day.

The armed servant guarding at the royal doorway bowed before me and I returned his bow. This was no menial, no one here was that. He was a loyal friend of one he now, since the accession, worshipped as Divine King. Probably as a lad he had played and grown up with the royal youth. But even the household servants, those who cleaned the rooms and who removed and washed the magnificent polished stone dishes after the meals, these also were no slaves, nor even "servants" as we enlightened moderns understand the term. People of the villages they were, mostly, not of an inner ripeness for the training of a scribe, yet quick, intelligent, loyal and always immutably cheerful.

I had already asked how they found their way into the royal service from the obscurity into which they had been born. Such as these, I was told, had, in the service of their local Lords, stood out from the others for the traits they manifested. So they were sent to the King, and went gladly. For here, doing what they knew well how to perform, they felt themselves kin to the priests in the temples. Were they not, too, serving a God?

"The older nations around us, to the East and South," my informant said, "these live by the labors of slaves. And one can well reckon that when Khem too grows old she will be fed and clothed by captive strangers. Yet may the Gods grant that this be still far off for our good land."

Except for the guard, there was little to distinguish the King's doorway from my own, except that the door it held had carved into its polished wood the royal name. It opened to me. I prostrated myself before it without first even looking into the room.

To a modern, reading this last bit, it will probably seem strange as so many of the things I tell. Was I so fearful of infringing customs? Or was, and am I, perhaps, not a true modern man? I can only answer that my gesture was born of the heart. I have never met, even among the Great Ones of my own day and age (and I have known a number), any who could inspire such a true feeling of reverence that involved me in no abasement, no violation of my consciousness of being a free individual and true man.

Yet before I completed the movement a voice, that I knew, said from the room, "Enough. Your heart is open to me, and your love is a precious gift. Yet here we may be all as men together, and as humble fellow-servants of the Gods we cherish."

Then a hand, the strong hand of the King himself, lifted me as before up to my feet. He presented me to an older man who was with him, the Prince Herutataf, his uncle.

"This Royal One knows who you are, and of your journey," said Menkare. "We waited for you."

Raising his voice he called,

"Let the object be brought in!"

Shortly thereafter the door again swung wide, and there entered four heavy, muscular men with poles over their shoulders. Suspended between the poles in a net of strong, woven fibres, was a great, rectangular block wrapped carefully in clean, white cloth. It was laid at the feet of Menkare, who was seated again as we stood on either side of him, I not yet knowing what was to be expected, except that I had been told there would be a writing.

The four men were striving for a grip under the corners of the heavy thing, that they might remove it from the netting and the poles. He stopped them, saying, "There is no need. I will not have it here for long. Then it must go back to the well-guarded store-room until I choose what I will do with it."

He waved them from the room. The elderly Prince, walking on the twisted strands of the netting, stooped to undo the cloth.

"Wait a little," said the King. "You found this under the feet of the Ibis-headed One in the Temple at Khemennu?"

"I reported so, O My Lord," replied Herutataf with what seemed to me no very good grace.

"I myself have thanked you, and thank you again." Menkare, it seemed to me, was slightly smiling. "I wanted this Stranger Among Us to hear it directly from the One who has done the Children of Khem such good service. But let us now look at it here together."

He rose and moved forward, and he beckoned me to join them. Then those two of the Ruling House of Khem undid the white linen together. The sunlight, striking into the room, lit up that on which our eyes now rested.

It was a great block of iron, highly polished, all its six faces inlaid with lapis-lazuli. This was a writing in the ancient, pre-dynastic hieroglyphics, closely crowded yet beautiful in workmanship.

Menkare read, and nodded. "Confirmation," he said, "of what comes down to us by mouth from the years of the Sons of Horus before the Kingdoms were yet united. Here, I will read it to you. It is not long."

The sonorous words of the ancient speech, always rhythmically balanced in the structure of their sound, rolled powerfully across the quiet of the King's room. Soon too they opened for me a gate of memory. In the "Book of the Dead," in the Theban recension, written down thus for all to read far later in the course of Egypt's time, they had remained essentially unchanged—teachings that some think were a foreshadowing of Golgotha.

". . . I am the Lord of those who are raised up from the dead, who cometh forth from out of the darkness . . . the sixth hour, which belongeth at the head of the underworld, is the hour of the overthrow of the Fiend . . . the strength which protecteth me is . . . the blood and the cool water. . . ."

So I learned now, seeing the aftermath of the finding, that the old rubric, telling of its finding in this Fourth Dynasty reign was truly copied, and *not* a figment of tradition metamorphosed in the telling.

"Let this be well guarded," said the Great King. "Let it also be copied twice over, once for the treasury of the Sun Temple and once to be joined with the other ancient Words of the God in the Great Book that we assemble."

He turned to me, saying,

"I know well the time is coming when men will no longer hear with certainty the voices of the Lords of Heaven. They will still hear and yet not know if it be Maat, or merely their own souls telling them that which they long to hear. Then in that time, which *has* to come as men descend ever further in their true being, unto Earth, these pictured words from the Ancients can be guides and servants to them.

"O Man of the West, where the desert will have blown its sand into the hearts of men, I have much to do and the time is short, so short for me. Only a few years left me, and the Soul of My People cries for nurturing. And always the outer tasks, the works of providing the gift of the Nile, the good water that is food as it is drink to our fields of grain. The priest-physicians warned me that this body soon shall pass and I must then go on working from the Palace of the Lord of the Dead, no longer here where my heart and will can work as seeds in the black earth of Khem.

"This seems to you like weakness in a King? O Son of my heart? No, I misjudge you, for I see you understand. I remain a man, though made less than a man and more than a man by this kingship. You know the sign in our writing, for "kingship," the same stout club that denotes the word for a slave.

64

Tell your great scholars that was no accident, but was done with knowledge."

Abruptly he turned from me to his princely uncle.

"Herutataf, you have the humble thanks of All Egypt, now and to come, and your name shall be remembered for what you brought her on this day. So leave us now, for I would talk further with this, my son."

He sat silent then, brooding, as the prince departed, and the silence continued a long time. I felt around me that which one can feel when sorrow and emptiness have poured themselves in to such a degree that there is room then only for a *lightening* of the heart. And the inner picture was a true one, for at last he smiled again, that faint smile with a look of inner triumph that one sees on some of his statues as they have been preserved to modern times.

In that smile, I could say, was gathered the feeling of power, of youthful force and reckless, hopeful life to which I made a reference in the opening words of this book. For the outer manifestations of all this, the great works of engineering and architecture going on all through the land were necessarily closed away from me, or rather, I from them. How I longed then, and still long now to have seen more. Yet even then I knew that the priest who had ordered me kept in this close confinement, was guided by true intuition. How else could it have been?

The few who knew the truth of my arrival, and whence I came, through Time itself, were inwardly mature enough to take it in their stride. Yet cosmic laws hold good even in the face of the deeds of modern man, and history needed to follow its course so that men might grow in the only way that could mature them—by learning through error. So I could not be seen, or widely known of. I could speak of the future only when the words of others made it plain that through their way of perception they knew of these particular things already. While with it all I carried always the knowledge that I was destined after my departing again down the time stream to be soon forgotten by these Ancient Ones.

Grateful I remained, however, for what *was* given to me.

And hopeful I remain, returned now to my own place and time, that the will of the Guide of Human Evolution may allow it that a little at least of what I was permitted to bring back from Ancient Khem may live for my brothers of this present day and age.

This King had found his Peace again, in the long minutes while I sat quietly before him. He looked directly at me now.

"The task at least is clearly outlined," he said, "and for that one must have gratitude. I would tell you a little of it, that you may better understand the shaping of these things.

"The men of my earth-age must be brought down to wakefulness, to outer, earth-based waking that can sense, not just the Gods at work but the true outlines of what They mold in all the earth and in us. Their souls, and this is hard for men, must learn to feel reality in what their eyes and ears, their tasting tongues and their very skins perceive. And for them this is not easy. For us, who have had the schooling since our childhood (the Serving Lords and all the temple people), it is not so difficult. But the Khemti, by their nature, live far far more in the *feelings* that these things arouse in them.

"They are like a sleeper in the cold desert night who, if one lays a covering over him, will respond with a soft sigh and a loosing of his body muscles, yet who never really awakens before the rising of Ra shall touch the skin of his closed eyes.

"So the Divine Ones, knowing the time for coverlets was past, sent them, in Their due season, a King of Power. The force of Khufu was so great he even dreamed he did not need the very Ones who had sent him. He warmed our sleepers, not by blanketing but by rough wakening and giving tasks until their blood was glowing and they did not feel the night."

"He has become remembered, to my time," I interrupted, "as a hard taskmaster, whipping the weary slaves."

"The joy of Set," the King responded, "is in just such easy lies. The Truth is harder to speak forth in words that can convey it. Harsh he was to those who are now my people. Yet none felt they were as slaves. Serving their King, they feel that they serve Heaven. And their sensing of this is true enough. For even if the force of his earth-body shall cut him off from

66

spirit-wakefulness, the Lord of Khem, still unknowing, is only the chief servant of the Company of the Gods, carrying *Their* will out into this earth on which he walks.

"Egypt suffered weariness, as an individual man doing a great labor will find his entire body-substance aching. Yet she too grew in strength, as such a man who labors grows; and she rejoiced in all her new life forces. So Egypt wept true tears when that Great King became an Osiris and could walk no more among his people.

"There followed him, Khefren, shielded and guided by the falcon. The tasks continued heavy and his long years were no joy to Khem. Yet under him, less by what he did than by what went out from him, the Khemti learned to know, at least in its beginnings, the soaring power of *Thought* that can remember an earth-experience, re-living what has been.

"He, like the other, had no place in his being for human feelings, that was not his task. Yet they were never evil, though I can believe that men in times to come will think of them as wicked masters of the Khemti.

"So, had you come to our Valley a month sooner, you would have been swiftly slain, by his command. This would have been not out of blind suspicion, but after learning, and clearly understanding who and what and whence you were. For human thought by itself would point to such a death as best for Khem and for our task among these people.

"I see you nodding assent. You had anticipated that. And even I, who had a different labor set before me from Khephren's labors, could see no other end for you than a swift death. Were it not that my years have taught me to be humble, knowing that the Counsel of the Gods is wiser than our wisdom, you would have lain now under some moist earth where soon nothing should have remained to mark your strangeness of body.

"My special task, O Child of the West who has become my son through the intermingling of strange blood-streams, I think you know my task. Tell me how it appears to you."

I saw this as a test of understanding. My thoughts, a mixture of the tales Herodotus had given and what I had been able to learn for myself of this man who literally towered as he sat across from me, were confused and helpless. Then an image shone into my consciousness.

"In part at least, O My Father," I said. "The plant that grows too quickly in its reaching for the light cannot stand against the North Wind."

"A good answer," he said gently, "and a good part of the truth. These plants need sun-*warmth* and my work, unseen, outside their comprehension, is to give them that. The outer labors, channeling of water and making Houses for the Gods, always continue."

"For the Gods, and not for the King's glory," something in me echoed, though I did not voice this.

"Not for the King's glory," he repeated. "Your unspoken word is true. The Gods require earthly houses here. In your time men will have forgotten this, yet the Spirit is no formless presence. To work on earth even the Gods require two things: a fixed place for their special in-pouring, and human vehicles devoted, by their own free self-offering, to the service of the Divine. So the temples must be, as the priesthoods too must be.

"If either become impure, and this too happens, then the Dwellings and the servants both are god-forsaken. Yet they are not left alone. Strong demons enter, in false shapes; and all things, outwardly, will still continue, but bringing evil. This is the curse of Heaven."

Then he was silent a long time. Finally I spoke again.

"Tell me, O My Royal Father, of the three Pyramids, yours building, and those two of the Osirises before you. In those especially My Age can see only vainglory. Yes Lord, I believe I know the truth of it, but it would be good to hear the words of you who know."

"Those three together," this was said in solemn tones, "show every earth-man to himself. Clothed in the warmth and the light of the sun and moon and all the stars, he stands on earth in thinking, feeling, willing. He is broad-based upon the rock itself. He only touches, at a tiny point, the Heights of Heaven.

"Yet into him there shine, invertedly, three pyramids whose substance is that very light and warmth. Their points reach through him, into the ground itself. Substance of far places, they nevertheless are his true being—Cosmic Man interpenetrating earthly man. When that goal of true interpenetration is reached, in fact, in every human being, then Earth's task is done. Geb, the Earth Father, can rest then awhile and the Heavenly Mother Nut can take her child by the right hand and lead him over the fields of stars to new work places."

There was a long hush in the room. When he resumed his speaking it was in a different rhythm.

"The Sphinx that stands before the pyramids? He needed to be there to bring men back to their surroundings and the tasks of the immediate, fleeting day. Bull, lion, wings of an eagle and head of a man. Who is that but each man, himself, that walks about, here and in every land of earth? He is, in his nature, three fourths animal. That these beasts wait on man for their transforming, they themselves will let him know in their good time.

"Meanwhile the Sphinx serves as balance to the other image. For those that know these things have always comprehended the fact that with every lesson, with everything that strives to raise man to the heights, there must be that which brings him back, which holds him ever to this earth that is his place of labor, schooling, growth."

The King dismissed me then, in kindly fashion. I was led out through another door, for the courtyard, I later learned, had become filled with men who waited in quiet patience with business for Menkare. Such as these, I was not to be seen by, for many were not of the inner palace circle.

CHAPTER VIII

The King's Judgment

Later, after I had been in my room awhile, meditating on what I had heard, having been brought there through small passageways that ran around the outer walls of the great house, the King's brother came again. I had not seen him since that first night when he had befriended me. He told me he had been at the limestone quarries, supervising the marking out of new areas of the mother rock to be loosened and brought to the River on sledges, for the building work.

"How I wish you could see these things," he said. "It is another picture of our living, the active work of many thousand hands, directed by the spirits of wise leaders who understand as well as measure clearly this rocky earth on which we live and into which we die.

"Tragedy it is to me, that you are here as, in essence, a blind man among us. You who have come so far, on such strange ways, can hear of what we do, and sense even more—since you know at least a little of the reading of hearts. And yet the colors, glorious and bright, of the black land of the valley and the red, high deserts underneath the sun of noontime, the laboring people, who find more joy in their hard tasks than you would dream could be, the mothers nursing little children, sitting in a patch of shade, the herdsmen singing to their flocks, the full, high moon shining on the white-sheathed pyramids, all of these can be for you no more than the substance of another's dream."

"Yet what would it mean," I answered, "to the men of my own time? For me a joy, yes truly. Yet I did not come for pleasure. I am meeting the Khemti, learning of the Company of their Gods. And these meetings, and even a little learning of what your least herd boys know—in these I think, can lie a royal treasure to take back into my Western Land.

"If I can convey to men even a little of your truth, your Maat, then the Lord of Death, the Evil One who goes beyond his proper bounds in my age, can be to a degree delimited in his power."

"Reconcilement to that which is, never supine but striving always to live to the fulness that the Gods allow, to labor strongly at that which They give us for our doing, that already is Maat. I respect her pupil," the Prince said. A modern man in these surroundings, I could only stare at the ground in embarrassment. He laughed a little, yet not in a way to hurt me.

"One of the Khemti," he went on, "would have acknowledged such a word as truth, without pride yet without shame at being told of it. Deep are the gulfs, and yet, O My Brother, we stand truly very close.

"But be glad. Today I bring you a gift of viewing, to see with your bodily eyes that which few are given to see. For the Horus Menkare sits in royal judgment, and only those who have direct concern with the dispute are present with him."

"How then shall I . . . ?" I interrupted.

"The King gave orders that I am to take you within the walls to sit beside a certain aged Sun-priest you have met. He, the Chief of Prophets, ruler of On, comes there when our Lord asks him, that he may say later whether the royal judgment was in truth the embodiment of Atum's will.

"I was with them when the King spoke, saying a true voice had told him your presence would serve Maat. 'This day's judgment,' he said, 'will find its way out to the people, and be remembered and then half-remembered, and then live as a lie through all the years of man on earth. Not for me does this matter, but for those who are to come. For men already older at their birth than we when we die, should have at least the boon of knowing without distorted lies what went into the forming of their being in ages past.'

"The old priest nodded at my brother's speech. He said, replying, 'A Greek wanderer who is to come, shall hear it and tell it further as a tale of weakness and the desire to please men. Our Kings are not Kings of weakness, though even Kings are men and as men are permitted to be weak in certain things —else the Gods who ruled here of old could have stayed and not left us to make our growth through meeting trials. Let the lie be corrected. By the time that is brought to pass they shall be struggling back to spirit-truth again lest they all perish. In the inverted mirror of the past they can find a little of that which men need if they would go on living.'

"But now come. The King's hour does not wait."

He spoke truly, for in the Hall of Judgment we could hear the chamberlain's voice, droning as bailiffs in all times have droned out the formalities opening a civil hearing or a criminal case.

In the tiny wall space, two folding backless stools had been placed ready for the aged one and me, and at eye level were slits through which we could see into the great room. The setting was far simpler than the court of homage I had seen. Only a few of his circle were with the seated King, standing grouped informally behind him. The parties to the suit were on their knees before Menkare. In a gentle voice he bade them rise and stand there facing him.

Where we sat, within one of the side walls, we were about on a line with the petitioner and his opponent and thus could also see the King almost full face.

The one who brought suit began speaking. He had been heard in the local court of his Delta city and found no satisfaction. A land holder and breeder of cattle, his claim was that he had supplied to the temple of the local God, cattle for sacrificing, and he had not been repaid. Until three years before things had gone properly, but then, he said, the gold had turned to promises of gold, and more recently to weak excuses and pleadings for delay.

Finally, when he had dared to bring his case before the judges, the elders of the city, they ruled against him and told him to wait longer.

"Why so?", the King interrupted.

"O Majesty," the wizened farmer answered, "I am a ruined

man whatever I do or do not do, so I will speak out. It is well known that our city's chief of priests is a man belonging to the King. His fathers' fathers' fathers came to our city from far to the South, in Narmer's, the Osiris Narmer's time and were set over us to rule us. Our masters they have remained.

"Now the Osiris Khephren, who sat enthroned, til now, upon that seat whence now you rule us, was a King as regardless of men as was Narmer, Smiter of Heads and Uniter of the Kingdoms. Our judges feared him more than they feared Truth, so they have *always* ruled against me, for the King's friend.

"Of you, O Divine Menkare, men already begin to tell strange tales. They say that you are tender unto men, and that you would be as a servant to your people. I appeal directly to my King, Lord of the Two Lands.

"My accountings through the years are with me. Let your scribes study these and see if I do speak the truth. Then rule for me. Give just judgment, O King.

"This man, this priest, this noble, is rich in houses and lands. I will take payment in those, their value to be assessed by the King's Servants."

The gnarled farmer, dried and burned dark by the sun, was silent. I glanced across at the defendant in this case. He was a handsome man, still young, and he was smiling. His bearing reflected utmost confidence. There were no marks of tension in him.

When I looked back at the King, the gentle Menkare had risen from his throne and drawn himself up to his full height. This, I can only report, was a height greater than the feet and inches of his body. He seemed to fill the great chamber, and the double crown on his head appeared to reach beyond the ceiling. His voice had the quality of thunder that is close at hand—though still it was no loud voice. I was seeing the King's anger.

"First, let this man"—he pointed at the cattle grower—"be well beaten here and now for profaning the names of the Osirises that have ruled here. It is not for the men of Egypt to judge their Kings. The Horus on this throne can still defend his fathers' names and keep them cleansed of all impieties. Then let my servants study his accountings and I will give judgment in this case.

"The Temple Priest" (I glanced at the young man, his expression was undergoing a sudden change from its happy smugness) "the Temple Priest will be heard if he so wishes. But the facts, or lies, in the case will be visible in the other's records."

"I would, My Lord, I would speak," he stammered, almost with diffidence.

Menkare nodded, saying,

"But first let the impiety be punished."

Then I saw what to me was a strange thing, though it was obvious that to the others in the room it was an occurrence in the ordinary course of events: the bastinado, as it had survived almost into modern times. The one who had spoken so boldly was laid, stripped, on the floor. One servant held his arms and another his feet. A third, brawny for one of his race, then beat the man as a naughty child is punished. This went on for what seemed to me a long time, until the one who had spoken so boldly was crying aloud from pain. Finally he who had ordered the punishment said, "Enough."

He turned to the young priest-noble, nodding curtly.

"O Merciful Ruler," the defendant began, "your fathers set my fathers in the office I now hold. We have been as good servants are, to all of those who went before you, and I, My Lord, devote my life to you.

"As to this peasant," he looked with venom at the man who, clothed again, stood in his place in silence, "he knows I would repay him in good time.

"My Lord is aware I am the custodian of the temple revenues. For His glory, and the advantage of the God of My City, I made a ship and sent it out to trade with the Sea People, out of the mouths of Father Nile. I desired to make an increase of what was given into my hands when my own father went, three years ago, to join Osiris.

"The building and the stocking of this, in the first year of my service, took all the revenues I had, and more. There were many men who were glad to be my creditors, men who know that the King of the Two Lands is as a guardian of my house. These men wait in calm patience, only this dull fool here became concerned as to his payment."

"What of the ship?", Menkare interrupted.

"It is gone these two years now. Soon I expect it back. Men from the coastlands bring me often reports from afar of the good voyage that it makes. A little more time, O My King, and this cow-herd will have his return, and with interest. Send him away from you, O Divine One, for now you know the truth of all these things."

"Now do I indeed know the truth of these things," was the slow-spoken reply from the Throne. "You, my stupid servant, are the greatest of all the fools that ever stood before me. Those men who 'aided' you have sold the ship and cargo long ago. They only wait to get from you the debt that you still owe them.

"When my scribes here have verified the other man's accounting, let this sum be charged against the foolish priest. He must pay. Nothing else were justice."

At this, the young man's expression changed again. His face contorted in unadulterated horror.

"O My King, my personal possessions are few and small, and even if I sold myself and all my family into slavery, the gold were still not sufficient. Be merciful, you who are known for tenderness and mercy. Be merciful, O Hawk of Gold."

"Let them both go out from my presence. I will hear no more foolish words."

At this dismissal, I watched the old herdsman's face. His enemy was humbled. I caught what was near to a grin as he backed from the great hall, while the other came close to stumbling, half-blinded from the shock of what had happened.

In the succeeding silence, the King's voice was heard again:

"Let the chief of my scribes follow that foolish priest and tell him that the sum he owes is on its way to him, in bars of gold from my own treasury."

The Egyptian impassiveness of those about him came near to being shattered. This, Menkare noticed. He spoke again.

"The Lord of Egypt need make no explanations. Yet I

75

would have you understand, since you clearly do not, so that in future you may have more wisdom:

"The claim was just. The Lady of Truth, Herself, would punish me were I not to honor it. Yet that fool *cannot* pay, and his mere degradation would leave my House the weaker and thus leave this Land the weaker.

"I depart now, for tasks more useful to our People."

He rose abruptly and swept out of the pillared room.

I wondered most—in all that I had seen—regarding the King's certainty that the young man had been robbed and swindled. In another part of the palace with the old priest, I asked him concerning this.

He shook his head. "No spies," he said, "had told Menkare these things. Yet you may be certain that they are as he said. You saw the Twin Uraei, the Serpent Goddesses formed of gold, attached to his forehead, gold-banded around his head as he sat in judgment. They are wise and far-seeing, those two, and whether he be wearing their images or no."

Proof? Evidence? In our sense, none. I can but point to some last poor remnants of such things still left to us, here and there: the intuitions that sometimes bring a man to the right place at the right time; the perceptions of a mother that reads in her heart things which a child believes it has well hidden; the inspired flashes that shine out, even if only rarely, in the work of a true poet. These things, or the powers that make a weak man great in moments of universal terror. We all know these, and many more, yet by our schooling we are taught to gloss them over as . . . as what? Let the reader supply his own answer.

The apparent contradiction between the King's verdict and his then meeting the judgment from his own purse still bothered me. Remembering Herodotus' tale in this connection, and the explanation given him: the King so anxious to cultivate good will that he paid so the man would not be angry at him— the nonsensicality of this was too apparent. I could testify that Menkare was no weakling. At the same time his relative gentleness of attitude and his feeling of a kind of personal

76

humility obviously were things that, in a King of Egypt were, to understate it, startling.

Once, a few weeks after these events, I dared to question him in private conversation. He told me it was all a matter of Maat, and would have left it at that except that I pressed him. With what, in us, would have been impatience, though there was only an almost imperceptible darkening of those serene features, he said:

"The debt was clearly just, and the cattle-man had need of that which was due him. My servant, the foolish priest, had nothing with which to pay. A public degradation would have been just punishment for him, but would never have brought the other one his gold. Also, the priest is in a way the servant of My House, and this is well enough known. So his punishment would not have aided Egypt.

"You, man of the West of a generation still long unborn, I know that your heart finds it difficult to grasp it. But I, myself, am Egypt! Since the Gods forced my head under the Double Crown of the Two Lands, I am no longer a man. I am both more than a man and less. More because there flows through my head and heart, and sits within my bowels, every pain and joy, each desire, gladness, need and suffering of all that lies between the Cataracts and the Great Sea. And I am less because, despite all the guidance of the Company of the Gods, each choice of path, each course of words and deeds falls, in the end, to me."

"Some of our spiritual philosophers," I said, "have held that in your World Age men were led, were guided and unfree."

"Guided, yes," he answered, "yet for those who hold the rule over many others, be they priests or priest-kings, guidance goes only as far as a forking of the paths. And *both* the paths appear, at first, as equally the right ones.

"I have heard it said by seer-priests that at the beginnings of the millions of years, before earth was the earth, even the younger Gods were once given a choice of following the Aton or of withdrawing that they might make things ready for the coming realm of Set.

"If this be so, and I have no reason to doubt it, then I dare not complain in my own heart, I who am more than a man and yet so far less than the very least of Gods.

"Also, I would not have it different. For the sun-wisdom in my heart knows well that in the time to come *all men on earth* will be faced with the choice of their own decisions. Yet this will not be until the Sun's True Self has joined His Soul to man's, become the Earth Soul that he might thus prepare, for a future still distant even from *you*, out of the old earth a New Sun. His Power, lent to all that worship Him in Maat, in Truth, shall make it possible for them to choose, in freedom, how and where they walk.

"But come, I would have you learn another side of how we raise and teach the growing children of this House."

CHAPTER IX

The Garden-Temple of the Young

Then he took me out across the open court to a separate wing of the building. It was semi-isolated and had a little inner court of its own. This was planted, in part, with palms, and a great sycamore had a place of honor at the center.

"Hathor," he said, "the giver of heavenly milk who is also the wise, loving Mother, rules here. The children know her, though their way of worship is their own."

Running about the court, in a wild game, were laughing girls and boys of varying ages, up to the early teens. The adolescents were covered, though the younger ones had nothing between their bodies and the rays of the high sun. Reading my thought again, he smiled and said:

"There are those that watch to see that these do not stay so, in the burning rays, too long."

Like a herd of half-grown gazelles at play, the children had been absorbed at first, and did not notice him. When he spoke the second time his voice carried to them. They stood still a moment, then smiling happily and without fear, they converged toward him. They stopped some paces from him and made a bow of reverence.

As they stood there, these children of the Royal Household, his and his sisters' and his brothers' children all together, he talked to them a little. His voice, always quiet, held a note of happiness I had never heard in it before in all the weeks I had been within sound of it.

"Live so, in joy and laughter, in your free hours. You serve the Gods thus, for in play, you grow. Your heavenly mother, Hathor, mother of us all, knows these things well and watches

79

over you. Her strength and gentleness flow into you, and build you strong and supple. See that you bring nothing here into her garden-temple that could offend the Lady of the Sycamore Tree."

As he paused in speech, one of the older children, a serious-faced boy, made bold to interrupt.

"What do you mean, O Father of us and all Egypt? You know we bring nothing here into this Court of the Sycamore, unless it is the cloth we wear upon us. And the servants see that it is clean and white."

I was watching the King's face and saw a slight frown come. It had disappeared before he spoke again.

"Do you leave your hearts behind you, neatly arranged like scarabs, on the benches in your schoolrooms?" he asked the boy, gently smiling now as he spoke. "You must show me how *that* is done. We all of us, I too, have much that is still to be learned."

The boy flushed as he fell to his knees where he had been standing.

"I beg the forgiveness of the Royal Horus," he murmured, kneeling there. "I speak only the truth when I say that our teachers have showed us that children's hearts as well as the hearts of men and women bear in them as inner substance that which later must be weighed against Maat in the Judgment Hall of the West—where the ferryman who looks behind him shall bring us all one day."

"Do they prepare you only for the after-life, then?", the King asked him. "What of the present day, of here and now?"

"Dear Father, do not hold my foolishness against them," the boy said earnestly. "I do remember they have told us that every heart bears in it active powers for good or evil. It is like Ra, the Rising Sun himself. It can, by what it rays abroad to others, bring life and growth and gladness. It can, if it should try to withhold its light, or if it ray out dark and evil things, bring sorrow, sickness, even death before death's time. And such things we must not bring into this place."

The boy fell silent. He was close to tears.

"Stand, and come near to me," Menkare said. So the child

80

rose and walked over to him and stood before him, cast down but without fear. I watched, and saw no signs of any trembling or hesitancy. I myself, in the circumstances, would have had to master a great deal to approach that King in such a fashion. For while it is a difficult thing to convey to modern people, the fact was that all of those of that time whom I encountered were, I can only call it *'formidable'* by our standards of experience, and their Ruler most of all.

He reached out both his hands then, placing them on the boy's shoulders. He drew him nearer, leaned down and kissed him gently on the forehead.

"You are my true son," he said. "You have learned well. Only remember that those of this Household dare not *ever* to forget the Teachings. This house is the foundation-stone of Khem. If it lacks in firmness, the whole structure falls. Those in this House are born to serve the Gods, and the Gods desire that this service be performed in deeds of Wisdom, Love and Strength for the helping of all their children that labor along our River, from the Cataracts to the Great Sea.

"Back now to your play. Let it be as though I were not in this courtyard."

I wondered at these last words. To me, the command would have seemed impossible of fulfillment. Yet in a matter of moments the children had moved off, shaped themselves into different groups and resumed their various games where they had left them.

The young voices rose from various parts of the area. And there was laughter, much running about, and splashing as some leaped in and out of the shallow pool, avoiding only those places where the lotuses were blooming, rooted in earth held there by copper walls across the corners.

Menkare watched them a long time in silence. I saw his eyes travel from one to the other, always observing and noting. At last he turned to me.

"These will do their work well," he commented,

"All of them, O My Father? you are fortunate."

"All of them," he answered, "because to each will be given tasks suited to the smaller or the greater powers that he carries in him. And the girls are the most closely meditated on. You know well that we trace our descent through the blood of the Mothers. Khem will stand or fall according to what those who bear her Rulers give to Khem.

"O, I do not mean just the wearers of the Double Crown. All the other Princes labor as hard as those do. They only do not have the load of utter loneliness the King must carry. They are spared that, yet in all other ways they bear great burdens also.

"Come, I will show you now a little of how they are prepared for later, adult tasks to come. The free hour will soon be over. We will wait in one of the places of instruction that you have not yet seen."

He took me through a small opening into another court. It was smaller, far smaller than the one we had just left. It held nothing but an expanse of smooth-raked sand, and was shaded by an awning from the rays of the direct sun. In one corner were coils of rope-like cord, and pegs and hammers.

The young priest-teacher waiting there bowed low. The King gestured. "I am not present," he said, walking carefully near the edge of one wall to leave foot-marks only on the borders of the sand. I followed, and stood at his side in a far corner. Then I saw that the sand had been slightly moistened— just enough so that it would hold marks made in it.

Very shortly thereafter all the older children from the Courtyard of the Sycamore Tree came in and took their places near the instructor. I had, for some reason, been expecting to see only the older boys, but there was an almost equal number of girls with them. Why I had thought it would be otherwise I could not exactly say, for we in modern times certainly give both sexes the same education. Perhaps it was a lingering remnant of notions about archaic peoples.

In any case, the King's intuition again read my question. In a low, conversational tone he answered the unspoken words.

"We want their wives, when their time comes for the men to do the men's work, to know what it is they carry on, even, when need arises, to take their places. Think back only to the Lady Isis and her rulership."

"O Majesty," the words slid from my tongue, for somehow one could remain at ease with him despite his awe-engendering qualities. "O Majesty, is not the story of Isis for you a legend? A *picturing* of high wisdom embodied on the earth?"

"That, yes," he said. "Yet has the Race forgotten that every 'Legend,' each symbolic tale, has at one time or other found expression in earthly, external life?"

"One or two true perceivers in our time," I answered, "have said as much. Yet they are not highly regarded among most of those who lead men's thinking."

He shook his head slowly and murmured, "A great grief, to hear your words. Where, then, is progress if foundation truths become forgotten and need to be re-learned?"

"Perhaps, Menkare, in the very re-learning, in grief and tears, by men no longer led about by Heaven."

He was very still awhile, then he inclined his great head.

"Your words please me. I think, O my son, that Wisdom, even when re-born as a helpless child in a far-off house, still grows to meet her tasks as the Race ages."

As we spoke thus, the lesson had begun.

"Remember," the instructor was saying, "the task today is the stretching of the cords, the laying out of the ground plan, for the House of Eternity of Him who has just become an Osiris. You know the dimensions of the Great King's pyramid. We have been there and made our own measurements. It is to be made smaller by us, in a proportion to be fitted in our place of work here. Orientation to the sun and stars must, of course, be identical. Now proceed to it."

Then the children reached into their garments and took out flakes of stone on which were written sets of figures. They conferred quietly together while two of the youngest of the boys present, having taken a long string, each by an end, proceeded to opposite sides of the courtyard.

I followed one as he looked along the wall until he found, cut high enough to be out of usual reach, and thus of any blurring, a sharp vertical line-mark made in the smooth surface of the wall. He held his end of the string to it and called out. At about the same time his fellow across the area did likewise. Two of the girls came running lightly, one to each youth. Both held lengths of twine with a pointed weight on one end. They looped the free end over the heavier cord that the boys were holding, each to his mark. These were a few feet out from either wall, and the pointed weights touched the sand, opposite to one another. The boys brought their cord down to the ground, touching exactly where the points of the weights had marked the sand. Others came and carefully pegged in the ends of the longer cord behind them.

"Being children," the King murmured to me, "they had been allowed the help of the wall in this operation that is otherwise done out in the open. You will find that the cord runs in a true North and South direction. Yet even the determining of that and its marking on the wall, they did themselves awhile ago, under that priest's direction."

All the activity was going on as though, literally, the King and father of their household were not there. That commands should be obeyed was not surprising, but I was, somehow, stirred again by the fact of their complete un-selfconsciousness. It reinforced my growing knowledge that, in contrast to the Kingdoms to the North-East, in Asia Minor, these rulers of Egypt, if not the folk they guided, were a young and virile race. Knowledge they had, and a priesthood with an accumulation of old wisdom. Yet they, these standing before me exemplified it, showed themselves as the children of a race of pioneers reaching out gladly into substantial tasks. They were in actual fact reaching out from an older, guided and dream-like consciousness, into a waking relationship to solid earth and earth-transforming labors.

This knowledge then was reinforced in me at other lesson periods that I attended. On the same sand floor wetted down to great firmness, the course of the Upper Nile was dug, and with amazing accuracy. I can vouch for that, since this was something I remembered at first hand, from time I had spent there "earlier," in the Twentieth Century.

The Cataracts were shown, and the rock formations on either bank. Then these same children had the task of determining how best, and with the least expenditure of labor, to cut in the mother-rock canals for the passage of the King's ships to Nubia.

Theoretically, by similar means, they studied quarrying. For this, small rocks had been carried in by servants. The young, future rulers of the land and its divisions then worked with chisels, smaller replicas of the great ones, and little wooden wedges soaked with water so that they swelled and split the stone. They had to separate out great construction blocks, always in miniature but with perfectly aligned sides and in true proportions.

It was explained to me that soon the older of these boys would be going out in person to the constructions, to the canals and to the desert quarries, there to work as apprentice-helpers to the directors of the various works.

"In this way," I was told, "they are able to start from the beginning with inner strength and balance, and a trust in their own selves. We *know* this plan is good, for it already bears rich fruit."

CHAPTER X

The Fields of Peace

In the weeks of this vicarious experience of the Teaching of the Youth, I had been seeing nothing at all of Nutka. In her own absence there was literally no-one I could ask about her. One thing I would have learned in these long days had I had need of learning it, which need I did *not* have: I truly, deeply loved her. What lived between us had rooted in something deeper, longer-lasting than these bodies that we wore.

If I had not been physically, as well as in my perceptions, exhausted by the fullness and variety of the days that passed me by so fast—even within the limits of one House, I would have lain awake, grieving. As it was, I always fell into a deep sleep in the grateful night-time coolness of that land. Sometimes I dreamed of a small hand touching mine. I would stir, come half-awake, shake my head and mutter to myself—whether in the language of these people or my own, I do not remember— saying, "It is, it can only be, a dream that I was having." And right afterward, because my whole self was weary, I was deep in sleep again.

Many of those days I spent in the Hathor Court, rarely with the King himself, but often with the brother of the King, the same one who had befriended me at the first. From him I learned that the King was leaving soon on an extended journey, first to inspect the desert quarries in the East, and then up the River, as far as the First Cataract.

Now for the first time I took serious note of the passage of time. Up to now, even within the spatially limited environment the days had been too full, too heavily loaded with impressions for this to sink in on my consciousness. I had to admit it to myself that I was now in a partially dazed condition. It was understandable enough. Here I was, a man of the Twentieth Century, not entirely typical perhaps, yet a modern man. And I was living close to the surging heartbeats of a culture unbelievably different from ours. True, there were likenesses, particularly, as I have said, to the vitality, the still-not-lost pioneer energy of the Anglo-American people. And the genuine preoccupation of these Egyptians with the molding and physical shaping of their environment—expressing itself in architecture and bold engineering works—that too was akin to ours. Yet the differences were greater, far greater in a sense than the scholars could have realized on the basis of their cultural reconstructions from the ancient records.

Chiefly, I think, the differences lay in the basic inner quiet, the so sure and so seldom disturbed spiritual balance that held them all, from King to the least laborer, erect in all of the vicissitudes that came upon them. And the impact of this, on me, came in the form of an inner dreaminess, a kind of tiredness, for I found the experience strenuous.

At the moment I heard the news of the King's fairly imminent departure, I came fully and harshly awake again. I realized with a start that I had made a definite agreement with the scientist friends I'd left at the First Cataract that if I lived through the experience I would return, if possible, in the way I'd come, at a time not exceeding that which—a quick reckoning showed me—had nearly passed already.

And the King was journeying to the First Cataract. I thought back carefully, and I could tell myself with certainty that one thing I had never referred to in my full and frank conversations with Menkare was the time of my again leaving his realm. We both knew that my going was a necessity. The incongruity of my presence in his house—dangerous enough, even with all precautions, for the balance of his Land—was something that had to be brought to an end within a reasonable time. And for my part, the whole venture would have failed of its purpose if I had not carried out its limited time-schedule and made proper contact with those who were waiting for me.

Yet we had not discussed it. But now Menkare was leaving for the point of my departure at the time when it was due. I could not conceive of this as any coincidence. I had to put it down, along with many other like instances I had observed, to that practical, intuitive perception that functioned for him, and in him, in all that concerned his rulership. Whenever I had referred to it, he always smiled that slight, almost gay smile immortalized in some of the statues of him. He would point to the Uraeus on his forehead, whether he happened to be wearing this golden emblem at the moment or not.

"I am helped, when help is needed, not for Menkare but for Khem and for the Khemti," he would say.

In any event, here it was. Without any semi-divine powers of intuition to assist me, I knew with certainty that I was leaving, and would be making the upstream journey in one of the ships of the flotilla of the King.

Nutka, where was Nutka? And why had I not seen her, except, perhaps, dimly in my dreams? I felt the need of help. I wanted to cry out to Powers stronger than I was. Yet something prevented me. I could have called on those known to us as the Gods of Egypt, for I knew by now that these, great indeed in their way, were nothing but members of that Hierarchy later called the Angels. Yet dared I ask for help for my poor personal self?

The King's words echoed in me "not for Menkare, for Khem and the Khemti." Was there not, however, Nutka to consider? I could ask for help for her, could cry for aid because of her. Even as I formed the thought I knew it was a sophistry. I was a lover who had lost his love, and I was bereft.

So I sat on my cot-bed in the Palace room that I had come, in my waking dreaming, to think of as "mine." My elbows rested on my knees, my forehead on my hands. My eyes were pressed into my palms. I was striving, a little too desperately for any good result, for some of the sense, of the feeling, of inner balance that flowed from these people all around me, tangible, almost, as the waters of a sea.

I heard no sound, no footstep. Suddenly, though, I heard a voice.

"Joseph, O my beloved Joseph, you strive well. Remember, though, that we are trained to inner calm from childhood. You *have* learned much, gone far in this little time.

"But now, stand up, and kiss me. And hold me close. Yes, hold me very close."

She was shivering. I had never felt this strong and lovely girl trembling before.

"It is nothing," she said, and then, "O it is everything, everything. It is like having your funeral rites while you still stand, warm, close to me."

Then Nutka, that brave daughter of the Khemti, dissolved in tears. For a while she stood, sobbing wildly, in my arms. The weeping died down, but there was a soft wailing, like the keening of the Celts. I could only hold her, firmly, quietly. Murmured words of love and comfort would have had no place in that room. Here was an elemental force that needed first to spend itself.

In time it did so. Wearily, but calmly, she disengaged herself. Without words she removed the clothing that she wore and entered the bed, beneath the sheet of fine, white linen.

She looked up, directly at me. In an almost ordinary tone she directed me,

"Come and lie here, quietly beside me. Our nearness is become too precious now to waste it further."

I did so, and prone, we held each other. In neither of us was there, in that hour, desire for closer bodily communing. We breathed deeply, and in unison, yet our breathing was a slow one, in a rhythm like that of a deep sleep. We spoke no more words to one another. We each knew everything that lived within the other's heart.

After a long time so, we drifted into an actual sleep. From this we woke with a kind of suddenness. Our dreams must have been good for we were laughing. Probably the laughter was what woke us.

"The present moment lives, and it too, somehow, is eternal. We two, we are the most fortunate of mortals, truly uniquely blessed," she whispered then. "Let us be glad of these things."

She was silent for an everlasting moment. Then she spoke,

and her tone seemed almost loud. Its happiness, its full, unblemished happiness was true and real.

"Come now, my truly beloved. I would have you through and through my being, in our bodies interwoven, as we are forever interwoven in our souls and in the eternal core of each of us that lives forever."

Her arms were around me like the caress of sunlight on my skin.

Before the morning came, we slept again. This time our sleep was deep, and without dreams. When I did finally awaken, memory came flooding back. So I half expected it would be as it had been before—an emptiness beside me matching the hollows in my inner soul where Nutka had been. Yet as I came to fuller consciousness, (I waken slowly), I felt her nearness. She was still pressed close to me.

I half turned, looked into her face, and she was smiling.

"It is permitted us," she said. "Do not ask how or why, but live with me and know me all these holy nights and days. Know my body with such knowing that you never shall forget. Know my life body too, my soul and all my being. Thus in me you know Egypt. So the Divine Will speaks, for its own purposes.

"At the same time my human self that serves Them half believes"—here her eyes sparkled again—"I am convinced that somehow my Beloved will not find their task a hard one. . . ."

She was going on in this vein until I closed her mouth with kisses.

So it came about that for my final week in that palace in Memphis, the City of the White Wall, Nutka and I lived very much as did the other couples of that ramified Royal Household. It is true that we could not join in the gay mealtimes arranged by groups that gathered under bright awnings on the rooftops, or in one of the larger courtyards. Our meals were served to us in the same chamber that had been mine and now was truly *our* room. I understood this, for the same reasons still held as before. It was not permitted that I mingle freely with any save the children. Those, even more than the children of today, were by their nature quick at the forgetting that was needed lest my visit harm the stream of orderly unfolding that was Early Egypt.

Yet there were a few adults, even outside the higher priesthood, that were permitted closer contact with me. The Prince, the younger brother of Menkare, the one who had first met me and had always been my friend, was permitted to bring his young bride to visit us. She was a delightful child. I use the word deliberately, for though she was of the years, and the growth, of a woman, she kept the impetuosity of those I had seen romping in the Hathor Courtyard beneath the great sycamore tree.

Not that her mind was undeveloped. It was supple and quick—always, it must be remembered, in terms of the early Egyptian mind—not abstract like ours, not "intellectual," but lively at the forming of themselves-living pictures that mirrored truth in unmistakable shapes. Yet she consciously lived in the outer moment rather than in inner dreams. And she was lively in her observation and in comments on all she had seen. From her I got, as from her husband, warm human affection utterly disinterested, concerned only with my happiness and well-being. And she gave me that which he, and even Nutka, could not give: vivid word-sketches of what went on in the Palace.

"Concerning you, I must restrain myself," she told me with a humorous little smile at the time of our first meeting. "I am to put no questions either to you or about you, on pain of fearful things: and I am never—this for me is the most strenuous part—to speak a word, even of your existence, to anyone at all. However . . ." she turned to Nutka as she went on speaking.

"However, little Sister, he is pleasant to be near. You are fortunate, though not so fortunate as I am."

Nutka sighed. It was a slight sigh by our modern standards, yet for one of the Khemti it was a tremendous showing of emotion.

"Yes," she answered slowly, "I am fortunate and I do know it. And grateful to the Ones in the Fields of Heaven and in the Land of the Unborn, who have permitted it. But come, let us now eat and then we will have the evening hours for talk together.

So we supped as friendly couples have in all the ages and the places of Man. When the servants had removed the plates and the little serving tables, along with the small remainders of the ample meal, Nutka turned to her again.

"Beloved, my Royal Sister," she addressed the Princess who sat looking at her, a little startled, with great eyes, "I pray the Divine Mother that when your time comes for learning how High Happiness is bounded, like a lonely mountain, by valleys of deep pain, she will be gentle and comforting as she shows you that which has to be."

"How mean you that, Nutka?" the girl asked in a soft voice.

"I mean," she said, "that soon my only Beloved must journey into the West."

At that the other girl's face was clouded. She rose and moved beside Nutka, crouched near her and seemed to surround her and murmured sounds of comforting.

For Those of Khem, Nutka's words of travel Westward had *one* meaning, "Death." For her and me it meant my journey back, through time, into the Western World. And yet, where was the difference as far as she and I were concerned?

It is so unutterably difficult to convey to a reader a true picture of these last days and nights in the Palace chamber. What I have just said gives a picture of sadness. Yet all through that evening, as through the whole week, our hearts were in fact rejoicing.

We were beginning to learn of the truths of Divine Love. While performing ancient natural rites before the High Altar of Life, whose priest is Death, we began to taste, at the same time, the sacrificial bread of Hotep and to know the peace given to them who have been allowed even a crust of that strengthening food.

This was a true marriage, and so that night and all the nights of my last week in Khem we had full earthly joy in one another. We gave no thought to boundaries of time, for we were outside time and lived in an eternal present moment.

Once, I remember waking in the cold morning, while Nutka still slept, and thinking wryly of Faust reaching his earthly ending when he had asked the fleeting moment to remain.

"At least," I murmured to myself, "for me it stays, unasked. And though for me too it brings Death in His essence, I am more blessed than that other modern was. I *have* fulfillment."

Nutka stirred and murmured then, but I gently kissed her back to sleep, holding her until her breath again was slow and even. Now I faced my fate in quiet. An inner calm was loaned me by those peaceful Gods of Ancient Khem, Beings that even slew, when slay they must, in stillness. Never unmoved, not unfeeling, they fulfilled the mandates of the Great God, breathing only gladness in the task, in any task. The priests described this by saying that Maat—cosmic law and divine necessity— was to them as is food to men. These "lived by Maat," and this was more than any mere abiding by the law.

So still today, and I note this with fullest gratitude of heart, as I sit in my New England room near a great University and write of these things between the conferences with the archaeologists and historians of the past, something of what They loaned me still remains like a taper's flame in my heart. The calm, the stabilizing quiet that the Gods and Men of Egypt gave me—a part of it at least, survived the whirlpool of that mechanized journey through the abyssal voids of time. I feel, too, that They will not take it from me in the years still left me for walking the earth in this body that I wear.

Without the help of that *God-given* inner balance I do not believe I could have survived my returning and all that this entailed. First there was the ever growing, and widely enough recognized, pressure of the increasing disorganization of our present life, social, political, moral, ever churning as do waters blackened by fierce line squalls. These are waters harder and harder for freedom-breathing souls to sail without capsizing. But most fearful of all was the shock of losing Nutka.

O yes, I knew, as she did. There was no evading of our fate. But this did not make it any easier. Sudden, unexpected death seems a cruelty to the survivor, when two have loved. Yet we were like two of whom one has an appointment, an irrevocable meeting with the executioner. And somehow that is worse. And the pain was, in a sense, doubled because we both—she there and I in this future-present—were *both* to be survivors. We lived in sensing our own and grieving for the other's pain.

Yet, as I said, that time, withal, was gloriously glad. This is beyond my powers of explaining. I can only note that it was so. If I am to die tomorrow or in a decade or so, I go with nothing, nothing but thankfulness for that which has been given me.

I had intended, here at this point in my writing, to sketch a vivid and objective picture of our culminating time. I thought to set forth every detail, small and great, of our outer and our inner living and doing. Yet I cannot.

I do not believe that it is needed for the conveying of that which Ancient Khem would give towards helping with the nourishing of our famished time. Nor would it be just to My Beloved to expose her so. Any who have experienced, whether through the years or for the briefest time, perfect earthly human love, any such men and women will know what those brief days and nights were for us. For the others, for those who have been denied this, endless volumes, Wagner in his music, the greatest of poets at their poetic heights, could not convey it. So who am I, a faltering time traveller, to try?

The Great King, Menkare, was wise and truly kind in the doing of what Maat demanded of him.

We were given no warning in advance.

We had had a night of fullest joy in one another, a joy that went beyond the interweaving of our blood and breathing. Our very souls, the vehicles of all our inner being were one in light and laughter. And the light was now no longer moonlight, but the light and warmth of Ra, gleaming down as on a high, grassy islet in the marshes of the Delta.

We knew we were still within our room in the palace in the City of the White Wall. Yet, we told one another, this is a perfect island, our own island set in the Fields of Peace.

"We, alive, have discovered the blessed Marshes of Aaru," Nutka whispered then. "Yet we are still alive, nor have we passed the Judgment Hall of Asr for the weighing of our hearts in the great Balance."

We heard footsteps then. We both heard them. Deliberately loud they were, that we might be warned.

We were sitting side by side when the King's messenger entered the room. Menkare had done us the kindness of sending that same brother who had first welcomed me and who had befriended me from the beginning.

The Prince's face was grave. His eyes lacked the impassive gaze that he, with all the Khemti were used to wearing even through great grief. They were the sad eyes of a *modern* man performing that which tore his heart. First he bowed low to us, as to a couple enthroned. Then he spoke.

"This man must go, to board the King's ship which waits for him now.

"No, Beloved Sister"—he anticipated her words even as she was drawing breath to voice them—"the Royal Falcon of Gold commands that Nutka shall remain, staying even within this chamber until it again be night."

He turned his eyes to me then, saying, "Joseph Aramath, it is a cup of bitter wine that the King's Servant brings you. I wait outside this doorway. Join me quickly." He withdrew on silent feet.

We had both risen. Our thoughts, will, feelings, were still one, as they had been before the footsteps came. With one mind we both knew that we dared risk no speech. Wordlessly, we told each other that in the time measures of the Eternal Stars this was a parting for a little moment, with God-pledged surety of being re-united soon. Only, we dared not embrace.

We looked long, each into the other's eyes. With a single will we both then turned away, she to face the chamber wall, I to the curtained doorway, striding through it.

The Prince walked close beside me down the passage, his arm round the small of my back, giving me, through it, the strength of his youth and his pity.

We walked to the ship, instead of being carried in a litter as on my arrival. For that too, I was grateful. To go with long strides, instead of sitting in a curtained captivity, was a help to me in my strange condition. For I was not weary, every nerve was alive. So the walking, an outlet for my energies, helped me to maintain the calm I had sworn to myself I would hold to until my departure from Khem. Soldiers surrounded me and my royal companion, less for protection, I guessed, than to screen me from the direct view of the occasional early laborers who were already walking toward their tasks. These troops were all from the local levies, for in those days the armies maintained by the King were composed of native Egyptians. They were not professionals, but drafted for a time, to serve under their local Lords. Only the Chief of the King's Captains, and one or two other nobles of the Court devoted their full time to military things. And those matters were chiefly the guarding of the borders, and occasional shows of strength brought from up or down the River to remind any too ambitious Nomarchs that the Lord of the Double Crown was lord indeed.

We barely spoke, that kindly Prince and I. I do remember asking him one question:

"You spoke of 'the King's Ship.' You meant one of the King's own vessels?"

"No," he answered. "My words stand. The King's own traveling ship. Something unheard of, for one like you, a stranger in our gates, to be. . . . But many unheard of things there are, connected with you, O my Brother."

"And few of the Khemti shall hear of them," I said, smiling a little. "While those that do, shall soon lose any memory of me."

The light of the waxing moon was sufficiently bright for him to catch my smile. I sensed his questioning thoughts, but did not answer. He, a true son of Khem, did not express his query.

We spoke no more until we reached the river bank, where three great Nile ships were drawn up along the stone quay.

"I will be in the second," he murmured then. "May your journey be in peace and may your landing be in peace."

CHAPTER XI

Up the River of Egypt

He left me standing before the lead ship. Sailors were out and on the deck, hands on halyards already beginning to hoist the great sail, a heavy task with only metal rings instead of pulleys for the ropes to pass through. Others were ready to cast off. The pre-dawn stirrings of the North Wind were rippling the waters. This wind, blowing powerfully, was to carry us up the great River, back to the place of my entry into the Land of Khem, the Country of the Black Earth.

Two silent figures, the ship's officers as I later learned, came ashore, bowed gravely and respectfully before me and beckoned me to come.

I was led aboard and aft along the deck, past a large cabin made of heavy curtains firmly fixed on a framework of poles. Behind this was another, smaller cubicle. Within it a lamp burned. A cot-like traveling bed was in the little cabin, and a small table beside it with fruit tastefully arranged on one of those gleaming, carved and polished stone platters that I had loved as things of beauty since I first had seen them, ages later, in a museum in the West.

The officers withdrew and I was still on my feet, in a kind of daze again, when I heard another step behind me. It was the Pharaoh's personal steward. He too bowed.

"Our King rests," he said, "and he bade me say he wished you to do likewise. He will have speech with you when the Sun is high."

I felt as though I would never sleep again. Yet I could not remain standing, for inner weariness, and soon after this man left I threw myself down on the bed.

Whether it was a power in that relayed command, or only tiredness that overcame me, I do not know. However, I was so soon asleep that I did not even hear the sounds of getting under way.

When I woke again bright light was streaming in under the curtains, outlining the borders of the little cabin floor. Hastily then, I washed my body in the water provided for me that had been placed, in utensils, in a corner, before my arrival.

My movements had been heard, and as I was dressing a servant came with food.

"Our Lord says 'Eat without haste,' this man told me, 'The day is still long.' "

So I did as I was bidden, breakfasting in leisurely fashion, and amazed, as one always is in such situations of bereavement, that I could eat at all, let alone consume the quantities I did. But our physical bodies have their limits, and when they need replenishing, their demands still take precedence.

When I had finished, I sat quietly. Memories of my Lady Nutka flooded my being. Somehow, and naturally enough in the circumstances, she, to me *was* Egypt. My eyes were half closed and my head was bent. I was oblivious of where I was. Yet I was not startled when I felt a firm hand on my shoulder and heard the voice of the King.

"She is, and she is not," was all he said, interpolating as he so often had, his words into my thoughts. I half-turned, rose to make proper obeisance. Menkare shook his head.

"No, Traveller who has become my son and whom I am so soon to lose again. In the time that is left us let us be rather as brothers, encamped in the desert as we make a short journey together.

"Was there ever such a journey? It is clear that there can never be another. For before we enter on the Mysteries, on all that which is the only clear and true and lasting, there is one word I must say:

"I know that you yourself are wise enough never to try returning. But I know priesthoods; and those who sent you are, I think, a kind of priesthood of your time, even though their Gods have left them and they worship only that which is dead, the mineral substantial. As I know such men they are persistent. Where they have made a small conquest they rest not until they have won more.

"These men will be tempted to send another back. Let them hear me when I say that if ever another vessel like your own returns, not only will the occupant be slain summarily, but his vehicle will be destroyed, be crushed to rubble. And I do not think those are so easily constructed, even in your World Age. This must be so, or else this stream of growth that is mankind now, would be polluted as yours is. Such poison, so near its sources, would be unpleasing to the Guardians."

"But if they sent one to arrive a dynasty later," I interrupted. "You, Menkare, said I would be forgotten as are even vivid dreams, forgotten still in your lifetime."

"So must you be." He looked at me, smiling a little sadly. "But there will be that put down in the hidden writings that those who guide here know, which will make certain there will be no such further transgression if this has not then already been, in other ways, prevented by the Eternal Ones who move in time as we traverse this River, up or down-stream.

"But come, into my cabin where there is more space for two."

Then there began a series of conversations, throughout that day and into the night, through much of the time it took us to return me to that sacred island known to later ages as Elephantine. There, I was told, my time disk waited, unharmed and under heavy guard.

Those dialogues we had are being recorded in full, for the scholars. Truly, that is all done from memory, as there was that in my environment which kept me from writing any sort of notations even when I was alone. Do not ask me what that was. I could not explain it. I can only say that it was most real, as were so many true intangibles in that land of strong forces unseen yet even stronger than the unseen warmth of its Sun or the North Wind's force that took us, swiftly, against the current, up the mighty River.

My memory, however, or rather my power of remembering,

was more alive and keen than it has ever been before or since. This too, I must simply record as phenomenon, without attempting explanations.

The conversations I will not give here in any great detail. Being one myself, I know my fellow Twentieth Century Man. That which the psychologists call our "attention span" is all too brief. Were I to tell all that Menkare said, it would simply be "long speeches," tiring the reader. He would put my book down, being no longer entertained. My aim, to convey only a little of that which was in the soul-mood of these people, would then be self-defeated.

Let me, therefore, only say that this King concerned himself the most with that which lay, for him, still in the future—though in our past.

"We have known," he told me, as he had before, "that the holy Sun, the Aton's Self, Source and Out-pourer of Life, would some day have to join himself to Earth. The Life of life must pass through Death, as in our myths (all of them mirrors of Eternal Truth), he passes each night through the Rivers of the Underworld.

"Yet to have heard, from the lips of one who also lives by Maat, of these things *taking place*. This is the greatest blessing given any King of Egypt, the greatest even though I know that soon this King will have forgotten it. For I know also that even when the memory of your speech is erased from my heart, the power of your word will live in me and help me in that which is my task as His servant.

"Leave me now awhile. I would give an Offering of Thanks to the Great God, an offering made without hands and yet acceptable. I owe Him the thanks of a child to an understanding Father."

I saw nothing then, of that King, for a long time. Yet of his Kingdom my eyes saw, perhaps more than at any time since my time-disk had whirled to a stop. For shortly after he left me, his ship-captain came to my cabin.

"O pale, Noble Stranger," he said, "the King's Majesty sends to tell you you may open, a little, these curtains on either side. Should it chance that a ship of his servants, from the places along our way, were to come near—he relies on your love and obedience (I use the King's Majesty's words) to keep your presence hidden."

The officer bowed and withdrew. And so Menkare, father of his Land, who had in this brief time irrevocably become my father too, showed me a last great mark of his kindness. For he knew well how deeply disappointed I had been to *be in* Ancient Egypt and yet see almost nothing of it.

As it turned out, the views being always somewhat distant, I cannot say that my visual observations added, or could have added, much to our modern knowledge of his realm. Yet the impressions were powerful, both supplementing and confirming what I had gathered of its inner essence from its leaders.

Being under sail, our ship, with the other two following, loaded with functionaries and administrative officials, avoided mid-stream as far as possible. Sailing as close to shore as the depths permitted, they thus had less current to contend with. So on one bank or the other, depending on where the strength of the North Wind was greatest, I was given unrolling panoramas of the ribbon of green that was and still is Egypt.

There would be clusters of mud-walled houses, with fields, intensively cultivated, extending an hour's walking distance up-stream and down-stream from them. Then another tiny village. Occasionally we passed larger towns, with the great house of the local ruler clearly standing out from the rest. At one or two of these I was able, even through my little "window" to note signs of excitement and great activity among the people.

The King's ships had been noted on their approach, and his local nobles were evidently not at all sure that they were not due for an unheralded royal visit. This would have been by no means something unlikely, for I had learned in conversations at the palace that in the time of the Old Kingdom at least there was little of the planned formality that later settled around the person of the Ruler.

Yet he stopped nowhere on his Southward course, reserving his inspections for the journey, later, back to Memphis.

Always there were ships on the River, and small boats of every description. Little fishing craft, formed of bundled reeds, moved in pairs dragging nets between them. Larger, broad-beamed boats carried produce to the towns, and not infrequently pleasure craft, ancient equivalents of the modern power cruiser, went by us, oar-powered, while we, with our great sail overtook others bound up-stream as we were.

None hailed us as it had been thought they might. But this was merely fortunate coincidence, for in those days any subject could claim access to the King. He could do so freely when the King was moving about the realm, and by arrangement when he was in residence at Memphis or in other cities where his own houses stood.

A gradual increase, beyond the usual, in the amount of shipping made me wonder, late in that day. Then I remembered, we would be passing Thebes.

Here our captain had evidently been instructed to avoid complications as far as possible. We stayed near the opposite bank from the great buildings. Yet even so, I was able to see a light, swift vessel, heavily oared, put out while we were still downstream and make for our flotilla.

When it got within hailing distance of our lead ship, the Lord who sat under a canopy in the after end was directed to proceed to the one that carried the King's brother. The visitor was further assured of prolonged royal audience within a few days, on Menkare's return journey.

From my cabin I could not see what took place next, but soon that second ship of ours detached herself from our fleet and made for the Theban landing, with the smaller boat following. Evidently a grave matter, though I, of course, never learned what it was. I knew that the King's brother would not lightly so depart from the planned journey.

This was the only actual "incident" that took place. Yet it, and the unrolling pictures along Egypt's artery of life, gave me again the impression of a *young* and vital land. The forms of their life were different from ours, and they literally "worshipped" their king. Yet in essentials these were a *free* people—we do not refer here to all that developed in Egypt through her later centuries. I felt a stranger and yet not a stranger.

On the second morning after he had dismissed me, the curtains between the two cabins parted again and Menkare's hand beckoned me to him.

"This night," he said, "is the night of the full moon. And before night falls our ship will be made fast at the island landing."

I bowed deeply, making a silent obeisance. There was, so literally, nothing I could say. He knew my sorrow as he knew my realization of the inevitable nature of that which was to be done.

Standing, as I was, just inside the rear curtain-wall of his cabin, I raised my eyes now. Before me was a table spread with a feast, and seats for two.

"Dine with the King of Egypt," he said, and his eyes were laughing though his face stayed grave. "This day we are of equal rank, and sit as brothers." And through the meal he spoke, with wit and brilliance. It was mostly of his plans for Egypt in the years still left to him.

He was convinced, and history bore him out, that his time was to be short. He was in no way bitter about it, or rebellious.

"If Kings rise up against the Gods," I remember his saying, "what is left of Cosmic Order, where then is the rule of Maat?"

True, he was already overworking and keeping too long hours. His body showed the strain. It is easy enough to see how the later Egyptians, of a time which had lost touch with inner realities, could only conceive of turning night to day for purposes of revelry and indulgence. Hence the tale they gave to the visiting Herodotus. That any man, even a King, would hasten his journey to the tomb for the sake of fulfilling tasks—this was beyond their compassing.

His main concern, as he spoke to me through that late afternoon into the sunset-time, was with the pacification of his Land, particularly the North. For the Delta Country still smarted under the Conquest, though all that had been carried through some hundreds of years before.

"Peace, under the Gods, with no more smiting of heads," he said. "This can only be through an opening of hearts to the true destiny of Khem. For this reason, besides sending out

103

the Teachers, I prepare books for men to read when they can no longer decipher the script of the stars."

The time passed swiftly. Then suddenly we heard orders given, the running of feet on the deck and the sounds of the furling of the great sail. Soon after that the ship-master entered and bowed low, reporting that the island was opposite us.

Under oars, the ship came to the landing. Soon we were made fast. Menkare was silent now. We both sat thus and I tried to absorb, like an emanation, something, even a little, of the power that was in him, nurtured on the true calm of inner balance.

After a long time he arose, still saying nothing, and went out on the deck. He was gone for what seemed to me many minutes, yet remembering back I doubt now that it was more than a few. Tension was mounting in me as I thought of my return, not just of the precarious journey ahead of me but more of that world of ours to which I was returning. I dreaded the turmoil and tension to which we are so used that we barely feel it. During my short stay with these ancient people I had so lived into their world-age that I could feel the roots of my being tearing, now that I was so close to leaving them forever.

I was like the one whose appointment with the executioner draws very near. Thankful I was again at the wisdom that had restrained Nutka from being here with me. Neither of us could have borne it.

There were footsteps now on the deck and though they were slower than usual I could still recognize the tread of Egypt's King. He re-entered the little deck cabin and drew the curtain close behind him.

"Farewells to the departing can only be pain," he said. Then he smiled a little, as he had so often done. "I feel in me, though," he added, "that even across the great bridge of the years we shall, if only in sleep, be close still to one another.

"O My Brother, O My Son." Menkare held his arms out to me. I wept as I moved towards him and he embraced me as a father might.

"Depart in peace," he murmured. "This must be our farewell. When we step forth I must again be Egypt, be impersonal, caring but for Egypt's good.

"The full moon is risen. Your vehicle is not far off. Be quick about what you must do. It is my will that those who, by Fate, must be present this night shall see what takes place happen with the swift confusion of a half-remembered dream."

With the saying of these last things, his arms had dropped again back to his sides. Yet, permeating me from that strange nearness to one of the Great Ones of history, was something I still can feel—calm, sureness, clarity, a quietness that quenches agitations coming from without. I cannot describe it better. I only know it is a reality.

"My King, My Father and My King," I could find no other words. He motioned me to go. Stupidly I turned first toward the curtain wall separating our two cabins.

He gently caught my arm and turned me about. Then I realized. I walked out on deck into the moonlight. I was alone, as the dying are alone even in company. I sensed one dim figure on the far end of the King's ship, watching me. Dimly I noted a few other forms at the dockside, yet the place was, by orders surely, almost deserted.

I orientated myself and saw then the strip of beach where the little boat had been that had carried me on that first night to the mainland and the presence of the local Lord.

Now I knew my way and walked firmly across the little island, not so over-built as it became in later times. Ahead of me, in the open space where I had left it, was my disk-vehicle, my vessel for voyaging in the time-stream.

One man only was now on guard before it. He was the captain of the little troop, he who had so bravely come to face an apparition from that disk when I had alighted there, he who had so wisely decided to spare me then the instant death that his general orders would have allowed.

"I am directed to hold no further converse," he said as he gravely saluted me. "Yet I am to give you the good wishes of my Lord, the Nomarch.

"Go in peace, and may our Gods ever guard you."

These were the last words that I heard in Egypt.

CHAPTER XII

Welcome, With Destruction

I swung myself onto the nearly flat surface of the disk and walked to the entry port. The door slid open under my fingers and I was inside, where cold light glowed.

I studied the dials and set them, consulting my written instructions for the return. Breathing deeply, I threw the switch that set the intricate circuits into operation.

Seated again in the exact center of the disk, where a compensating arrangement of gears kept me from spinning with its ever faster motion round me, I was physically stable. Yet, as before, on my "outward" journey, I soon felt my consciousness slipping away. The process reminded me of nothing so much as the old-fashioned ether anesthesia that one encountered in hospital operating rooms in the days of my youth. There was the similar glaring, aseptic-seeming light overhead, the hum as of motors. And while I was seated instead of lying prone, I found myself half-looking behind me for the masked and covered surgeon and his operating team.

At this point, however, there was an incongruity. I almost leaped from my seat—which would have brought the whole thing to a quick and fatal end with the automatically-set machine arriving at its destination in the present and the pilot, or rather his well-blended ingredients, spattered evenly over the inside walls of the great disk.

What I saw (I should say "seemed to see") bending over me, was the form of the wolf-headed Wep-Waat, the "Opener of Ways"! Shuddering at the apparition, I still managed to catch myself in time. My last thoughts were of the trust and devotion that this divinity inspired among those whom I was leaving,

106

and how they addressed themselves to him when going on a journey.

The guarding soldier's words, in the ancient language, re-echoed in me then and I relaxed, murmuring something about these having been powerful words indeed.

With the infinitely gradual slowing of the fantastic whirling speed around me, my consciousness, as it had done before, came slowly, slowly back to me.

Then, as the spinning thing was definitely losing its momentum and I realized that it must be becoming visible to any who might be watching from outside, there were new and strange sounds, ominous to me. I heard heavy crashes, as of explosions, at irregular intervals, and they seemed to come from all directions.

The disk itself began to tremble and appeared to lose its equilibrium. I couldn't fathom it. Was something wrong with the machinery? I was sure at first that some part must be malfunctioning.

The turning was close to coming to rest. The shocks and the constant vibrations were worse. But only as the sound penetrated through the relatively thin walls of high-tensile steel did I realize what was going on. An artillery barrage! And I was not merely in the line of fire but definitely in the area on the receiving end.

A fitting and symbolic welcome back to modern times, I thought ruefully. I was about resigned to the venture ending this way, when the disk, as far as its own process was concerned, was still.

At this point I began to function normally. Had I not done so, I would not have been here writing this. With no delay, I jumped from the seat, stood up and slid the entrance panel open. Climbing the few rungs that took me up, I raised my head outside.

There were shell bursts all around me. Elephantine Island was under artillery fire, saturation fire, from the shore. I could not fathom what lay behind it, but I did not stop to think. My party of scientists could not possibly be anywhere near, so, turning and dodging I made a fast broken-field run across the little open area and headed into the ruins. Their heavy masonry, suffering under the fire of what I decided must be light field-pieces, yet offered a little shelter. I headed toward the side of the island opposite from where the shells were whining in from.

On a piece of high ground that happened to have no obstructions between it and the open space where I had been encased in spinning steel, I turned for a final look.

The time machine was gleaming now in the early sunlight, and while I looked a shell made a direct hit. So strong had been the construction that the thing did not disintegrate to rubble. But it was deeply indented, and twisted out of form. Another shell came down, this time uncomfortably close to me. I threw myself flat, until the fragments had ceased flying, and then resumed my run.

Soon I was at the river's edge. The Nile was rising, and the current strong. I let myself down into the muddy water and drifted, gratefully, past the far side of the island. Fortunately, as readers of my earlier books know, I've always been a good swimmer. So, saving my strength and not at all anxious to come to any shore too soon, I gradually eased my drift out of mid-stream toward the shore.

I saw no soldiers or civilians along the banks. For that matter I had seen no one on the island. I suspected that the occupying troops had cleared out early during the barrage and that whoever had ordered it was wasting ammunition. But that was no concern of mine. At the time I couldn't even figure out what the war might be about. Only later did I learn that the trouble between Egypt and the Sudan had developed into military action in the relatively short time I was gone and the Sudanese were endeavoring to get themselves a foothold below the First Cataract.

Now, around a bend I saw a little village, a clustering of cultivators' huts. It was on the nearer bank, and as far as I could tell it appeared peaceful. Yet when I clambered up out of the river, stark naked as I'd made myself at the start of my long swim, two husky soldiers of the Egyptian Army, covered by a third holding a rifle at the ready, ran out of the nearest house and collared me.

My only-fair Arabic was enough to keep them from shooting me on sight. They had been watching me for some time, they said, and only wondered at an enemy agent taking this swim in daylight.

I managed to acquire some dirty clothing to cover me before I was taken to their superior officer. Him I was able to convince that I most probably was one of the mad European archaeologists, who had, somehow, been overlooked in the general evacuation.

Without too much trouble I got myself shipped, as a prisoner, on the train for Cairo. Glimpsing the Gizeh pyramids from the dusty window of the coach, the nature of this arrival: a perfect and demonic caricature of my recent earlier entry into Egypt and the down-river trip, struck me with force.

In Cairo, the Government people were most apologetic. Their top brass had, of course, been let in on the nature of our attempt. Otherwise there would have been no way of getting the time device into the country and setting it up. At the time, the Sudan crisis had been in the air but had not seemed too potentially dangerous to anyone.

The machine and I had, of course, disappeared. Then the shooting war began and the general in charge on the border had summarily bundled out of his area our whole group of scientists. The original plan had been for them to stay directly on the spot—for one thing, there was always the possibility of an emergency, anything unexpected, forcing me to return sooner than the scheduled date. For that reason alone it was essential that the space where the machine had rested be kept clear at all times of any obstructions.

Our people, forced to remain in the capital city, had been frantic, particularly as my arrival time drew closer. They were helpless as, with the enemy showing unexpected strength, nobody in power felt any inclination to bother with mere scientists, much less to allow a party of American civilians back into the combat zone. Our State Department, which also knew something of the project, had too much else at stake to intervene on our behalf.

So my colleagues were incredulously delighted when their bedraggled traveler was ceremoniously returned to them at the local military police headquarters. The next concern was the time machine itself.

Elephantine Island had been occupied by the enemy soon after the laying down of the barrage through which I had escaped. By now the place had again been recaptured by the Egyptian forces. Through the personal intervention of the Head of the Government, who knew some of our scientists and valued their friendship, it was possible to have one of the engineer officers with the front line troops detailed to make a full report on the condition of the vehicle.

When this report came in and was passed along to us our engineers and physicists were in despair. The internal damage to the time machine was irreparable. Any further such fourth dimensional voyages would require the construction of an entirely new machine. This meant special alloy steels rolled and machined to tolerances that were infinitely close to zero. It meant metal work and fabrication by craftsmen of such a degree of skill that they are watched as closely as any uranium stockpile by the F.B.I.

Not only are astronomical cost figures involved, as they were in the original project, but with the increasingly threatening international situation it is most doubtful whether the men, let alone the money, will be released for a duplication of the project. Originally our Government had rather reluctantly allowed it, regarding it as interesting to the highest degree but of no value for the cold war. It had finally been sold to them on the basis of a regaining, in a big way, of scientific prestige. Yet this purpose had, of course, now been accomplished, and their point of view was lately expressed as, why bother any further?

So I personally am convinced that at least in our time the project will not be taken up again. As for the future—who knows? If our whole technological "culture" breaks down, as it is almost sure to do in the event of full-scale war, no one will be left who is able to do it. And in much later times it is historically certain that my whole actual experience—if the tale survives in any form, will be regarded as no more than another of the fantastic legends of the *naïve* ancient peoples.

Should my words survive, and should such a machine ever be built again, I warn the riders away from Ancient Egypt. There is no question that that King's threat would be carried out. The traveler would be slain on sight and measures taken to annihilate his vehicle. And what other ancient culture is there, that we know of, with sufficient social stability to give a time traveler even a reasonable chance of debarking, making his investigations and getting back? True it is that the sardonic, sophisticated Romans of the Empire might receive such a one and even turn him loose again. But that the data and observations he might bring from an already well-documented and almost familiar period would be worth the expenditure and the human effort involved is, to me at least, doubtful.

Yet these are, in the nature of things, empty, abstract speculations. For our contemporary world, this journey back into the past is a closed chapter.

All of you have read, first the excited newspaper accounts and then the stories in the popular news weeklies, and feature articles everywhere. It is amusing to recall how for the first day the sensational papers in our big cities had it as an exclusive story, the more reputable dailies unanimously refusing to credit it. And who can blame those good editors? The thing *was* unbelievable. Yet, as we know, it did happen.

The full reports, the scholarly material, all this is, as I said earlier, still to come. Those men, and rightly so, have always worked unhurriedly. They are the ones who would lay sound masonry, and well erected, into the structure of our human knowledge, a structure which, if they are fortunate, will last far into the future. These scientists are, in a way, the equivalent of the calm, careful builders of the ancient pyramids. May their building last as well as had the work of their old predecessors.

The tale that I have tried to tell is of the *human* aspect of the adventure. This, not for the adventure's sake but because I believe, nay I know, that the intangibles that I brought back are potentially among the real treasures that our times, or rather the *people* of our times, can have to spend and yet to keep while spending.

Never, not ever, is it thought that they might in any way take even part of the place of the mighty spiritual treasures given to us and not given to the Ancients. We, by the Will of the Creator, with Whom the Redeemer, by His Own Words is One, are given "the power to become the Sons of God." Yet how many are there who have regard for these things?

No, all that Ancient Egypt has to give is, to put it deliberately in its crudest form, that spiritual essence which, in our troubled times, would make all "tranquilizers" unnecessary.

Here, from a certain point of view, my story might be ended. Yet out of regard for Truth Herself, a mighty Entity that those who have even briefly glimpsed her must ever after strive to serve, I am forced to carry my narrative a little further.

CHAPTER XIII

Hotep

In the first few of the many months since my return from the past, and even now in the relative peace of a quiet valley near the Connecticut River where I am finishing this manuscript, I was kept so busy that I had little time for personal sadness.

Sadness was always near me, though, and flooded over me in every brief moment that I was alone. It was not based on the obvious things. True, I sorrowed for those I had come to love, and most of all for Nutka, whom I had loved so briefly in those weeks stolen from time.

The focus of my grief was stranger than that. Nutka, the love of whom I only grew fully to realize in that bitter time of the ending of my stay there, was now present in my consciousness as embodiment of the Soul of Egypt. Her memory haunted me. This is an over-used and much abused word. Yet taken in its primal sense it is the only one to describe those worst weeks and months after my coming back.

I tried to imagine how, for even a part of that short time I could, even to a slight degree, have considered her as no more than the sharer of a joyous and, for our times still at least technically unconventional human experience. I had known Egypt, and only knew I knew her when I was losing her. How could I have been so unaware?

As I have written, I was too busy to come even near to losing my mental or emotional balance, although this could easily have happened had there been less outside calls on my energies and time. But even as it was, friends grew concerned about me.

Asking of Egypt, they would instead be told, and repetitiously I fear, about the tenderness and grace, the joyous calm, the ever-present quiet gladness of my Princess, of Nutka who had been my bride.

Finally one whom I will not name as it is better for his work that he should not become involved with me in these things, spoke to me severely. He is, in my terminology, one of the "better sort" of psychiatrists, neither over-concerned with one's sex impulses nor desirous of remolding all his patients— and the entire Folk if he can get his hands on it—into a grandiose pattern of some group conformity, a negative peacefulness.

Dr. X (this cliché should be a safe enough designation), took me to task one day.

"You, Joseph, of all people, know that my personal dream is of at least a slight degree of a restoration of the individualism, the many personal quirks in many men, that made this country great. I am happy to allow for oddities in my own patients, peculiarities even that if unchecked in their own clientele, would drive half my colleagues certifiably mad themselves.

"All our truly great men had great peculiarities. And while I can't expect my patients, or my friends, to become great thereby, I never thwart such traits unless they become too dangerously strong. For who knows what the "odd" man, left to flourish, may not yet have, to give his fellow men?

"But you, Joseph—returned from an adventure no man has had, or is likely to have again! Sensitive and perceptive to boot. One asks you reasonable questions about that ancient people, and you reply like some moon-struck, pubescent boy. You're living in a bodily image. Not only have you lost touch with the Soul of Egypt (O yes, you answer technical questions very well, and still please the research people), but you've *lost* the inner truth and reality of what you've lived through.

"You sit and stand, you eat and sleep, and any half-awake observer would know you're just pre-occupied with dreaming of a girl."

I had no answer for him, for I knew that he was right. I told him so, but I couldn't change myself.

O, I tried. I tried in every way, by logical thinking and by the power of prayer (neither of these being antithetical to

114

the other and both being paths to the truth). Yet there was no help for me, and I could not help myself. There was only one image, and Dr. X was right. It was, or at least had become, a physical image.

The archetypal world was a dead world for me. I stayed what I have always been, a believing Christian, if not orthodox. Yet these spiritual truths were like abstractions for me. And the powers known as the Gods of Egypt, angelic helpers of mankind along the path of growth, Powers whose reality I had experienced at first hand in that sojourn in the past. These also were as though they had never existed.

I lived in emptiness. I *was* a walking emptiness. Only in the great woods on the crest behind my river-valley house did I find any peace at all. The elemental powers of natural growth that lived and worked in those tall, quiet trees, They somehow gave me help, though all unknowing upon their part or mine.

The stars, where Nutka had said I should seek her, these remained abstractions to me, no more than little points of light.

I began to look for death. Not suicidally ever, but with great longing for the time when death should come in his due season.

Then one day, unexpectedly, Dr. X arrived again.

"Joe," he said, somewhat mendaciously as I discovered later, "I want you to help me. There's a patient in my hospital, been unconscious for several months, not unconscious exactly but the nearest thing you could call it is a very, very deep sleep condition. She'd been there under treatment—never mind for what, nothing serious, and anyway that doesn't concern you. Then suddenly one morning she didn't wake up, and she wouldn't wake up.

"Yes, I said 'she.' It happens to be a girl but that isn't the point. The point is nobody can wake her. I could use drugs but I'd rather not. There's too much we don't know about the human entity. I think that different people embody different forces in their—call it in their vitality. If I can find the right person something might happen, in a healthier way than it otherwise would. I've let things slide because she stayed well enough nourished with tube and intravenous feeding. But lately she's begun, physically, to show signs of sinking. So I want to try a dozen or so more people on her, try their nearness, that is, and if it doesn't work I'll shock her back to consciousness with drugs."

Of course I couldn't refuse him. We planned that he would stay the night with me, and the next day I'd ride with him, down the Valley to his hospital, which is in the outskirts of one of the big cities near the coast.

Of course I dreamed, waking and asleep, all that night, of Nutka. I was so constituted at that time that it could not have been otherwise. Supposing she is short and dark, and even a little like her. Could it be? I asked myself this and similar things. Dr. X had ruthlessly cut off any further questioning about his patient, so indirectly that left my fancy plenty of scope.

I looked haggard the next morning, and he commented on it.

"Do you want my help, or don't you?" was all I answered. So he grinned maliciously and went back to his ham and eggs.

Finally we got into his car. I was in such an inner state that the autumnal colors of the valley meant less to me than a gallery of modern abstractions. I had eaten almost nothing. Yet I was still not conscious of any hunger when we drove in to his grounds and left his convertible at the front door.

His resident doctor got hold of him and plied him with some problems that had arisen overnight. I sat in the comfortable, living-room-like downstairs lounge, not asleep but not conscious of my surroundings, though I had always enjoyed the place when I'd seen it on previous, social visits to Dr. X.

At last he came back, serious-faced, and beckoned to me.

"I shall use sound," he said, as I walked with him through the corridor. "It's what I've done on the earlier tests, a deep-toned gong to bring her, physically, as close to the threshold of waking as can be done by natural means. She ought to respond, but she doesn't.

"I'll strike it a few times, and then I'm going out of the room and leave you with her. Talk to her in any way you want to. The point is a focussing of your personality on hers.

"And, Joe, don't be disappointed if nothing comes of it. She's sunk very low in her vitality and may never. . . . Frankly, I'm using you because of the state you've gotten yourself in: that intensity of longing, it just might be of some use here."

I nodded, making no answer. My dreams of the impossible were glimmering. I should have realized there was a good, objective reason for my being brought into this. But my face, I believe, was impassive as I followed him into the private, corner room, expecting nothing.

Before me, on the white bed and well blanketed, lay a slender little blonde. I heard him murmur "blue-eyed." It was a type that had never interested me particularly.

She was very young, about nineteen, I guessed, and later found that I was right.

Dr. X said nothing further. He beckoned me to a chair close to the bed, closed the door to the hall and walked purposefully over to an old oriental gong on a side table. He struck it three times and then left the room, closing the door behind him.

The vibrations of sound continued for, what seemed to me, a very long time. I saw her stirring slightly, and saw, or fancied I saw, an expression of annoyance pass over the childlike face. She was like a sleeper disregarding the alarm clock that would call her back from rest.

There was absolutely nothing to suggest my time along the Nile, yet I was moved to greet her, to call out to her in an ancient morning phrase.

"Ra em Pet," the Sun is in the Sky, I called out to her in the tones that I had often used with Nutka when it was wiser that we sleep no longer. Then I sat shivering, not with fear but with wonder. I shivered in that warm room, though only briefly. For her eyes came slowly open, and they were a delicate, a tender blue. She said only one word, in a tone of questioning.

"Weben?" He rises? She who, as I verified later, could have known no Ancient Egyptian, answered me with what had always been Nutka's question in those moments.

117

"He is already far, in his day-boat across the sky," I replied in the same tongue, as I had always answered Nutka.

This girl before me, here in Connecticut, shook herself a little and said, in modern English:

"Then it's time for me to be getting up, myself. I've had a long sleep, a very, very long sleep."

But when she tried to raise herself, she fell back, murmuring something. I caught only, "so weak and faint."

I urged her to lie quietly a little, seeing in her eyes, as I spoke, that she was looking at a stranger and was startled.

I ran to the door and called to Dr. X who had been glumly pacing in the hall, head down and both hands buried in his pockets.

"Hurry," I said. I still remember his startled expression.

"What. . . ."

"No time now," I interrupted him. "Have you got stimulants, something for her to go on?" Then he went into action, and motioned me out.

I went without reluctance. Obviously I, a stranger, couldn't be of any more help just then, and actually I was beginning to feel a kind of delayed shock from the whole thing. Somehow I found my way back to the reception room and sank into a deep chair in a sheltered alcove part.

I found myself repeating those short phrases. The Ancient Ones were never redundant of speech, of course they weren't. But that isn't the point right now, and you know it, I interrupted myself. What you've got to consider is how, how can this be?

"And it isn't the how of it either," I found myself saying half aloud. "The fact is, nobody else would have or could have. . . . The same words, even the intonation . . . words, it was only *one* word from her . . . but *the* one word . . . you're strangers though, you both felt that as soon as she was really awake."

Then, and I am not ashamed of it, I fell to weeping. And the next thing I knew I was looking up to see Bill, Dr. X, standing over me, smiling a little.

"Easy, Joe," was all he said. And a little later, "I can imagine it was a bit of a shock. Suppose you tell me about it, how it all happened."

"You'll never believe me, and I have no witnesses," I answered him, rather bitterly.

"By a quirk of circumstances, you don't need them," Bill said, startling me. "Her people could afford it, and they had asked me to do *anything* I could, so for a good many weeks this room's been wired just in case she might have said something in her sleep, in the times she was alone, that could have given us any clue, that might have been of help in bringing her back. She didn't, but I kept the tapes running on an off chance, and left them going during the times I've had various people in as I had you today. I've already played it over, so I know how you spoke and how she answered.

"When I asked you how it happened, I meant *how?* What made you try just those words?"

"What made me try them? I don't know, I just don't know. That longing that you spoke of, I suppose." I went on to outline what my thoughts had gone through a few minutes before. And told him how it was a wake-up formula between Nutka and me, and how this girl now had answered me with Nutka's answer.

He interrupted me then to say that decipherable use of very ancient tongues by mental patients in states where they were not conscious of themselves was a phenomenon that had been definitely observed (though, of course, not explained) in hospitals.

"Not that she's 'mental,' " he added. "Let's have that clear. There were a few personality quirks that bothered her as much as they did her people. She came here of her own accord to see if we could get at the root of them. We were, frankly, getting nowhere and then—now brace yourself, Joe—it was just at the time, to the day, when you left your engineer and archaeologist friends on Elephantine Island to go into that time machine, that she fell into this sleep.

"Don't ask me to explain it. Obviously I can't. But the records show the coincidence in time, and there it is."

We didn't say much more just then, and after all, what

could we have said? Nothing that made any sense. So we left it, and he made me come with him and finally eat some breakfast. I surprised myself by eating quite heartily.

We talked of all kinds of other things. Only once, and with a glint of mischief in his eyes, he referred to the girl in the corner room upstairs.

"You'll be glad to know that up to the limits of what I can allow her at this point she's taking food with pleasure too," he said. I made no answer and he began talking about the up-coming election campaign in the State.

I listened as long as I could bear it, and then broke in.

"Don't tell me the issues mean that much to you," I said irritably. "I know you better. And I don't need psycho-therapy.

"I've got to see that girl again. When can I? Also, you might tell me what her name is."

He grinned at me and said, "Sorry old chap. It will probably sound like an alias to you, at this point, but it isn't. Just an ordinary name, Mary Jones. And you can see her now if you want to. Matter of fact, she's been asking about you. She wanted to know who that kind, older man was that was in her room when she woke up. 'He seems sort of nice,' she said, too; and I'm not making that up.

"Well, I told her enough about the recent months—as far as she was concerned—to give her the general pattern. I explained how I'd been trying different people, to get her awake. I said I'd chosen you this time because you'd had a personal loss and I felt that the very intensity of your longing just might. . . .

" 'And it seems it did,' she broke in. So it makes it easy enough for you to take the story from there.

"Another doctor would probably say to give her a chance to build up physically first. But Joe, I'm afraid. When she goes to sleep, as she must, soon, she might just slip back and get away from us again. I want her anchored in the here and now, and you're the one that can do it. So don't be afraid.

"Only, if she seems to you to be getting too much, in terms of her physical energy to take it, that is, push the button that calls the nurse. I'll be nearby, and right with you if you need me."

So we went back upstairs together. I'd find it difficult if I had now to give an accurate picture of my feelings in those minutes. I was rather numb, more than anything. Had the impossible happened? I know that's a cliché, but I haven't any better words for it. That, mainly, was what kept going through my head. In my heart and will, I was weary. All this couldn't be, and yet, and yet, there had been that exchange between us.

Inevitably, when we got to the door in a few minutes, I walked in without halting or even slowing up. For my own sanity's sake I had to find out more, and it *couldn't* wait. I think Bill had sensed that, and it was one reason why he had stretched a few points, medically, and let us get together again that soon.

I was reassured when I looked over to Mary. She gave me as heart-warming a grin as any nice nineteen-year-old might give a man in his forties.

"Hi Joe," she said. "I'm going to call you that, and you'd better call me by my first name even if we haven't been 'formally introduced.' "

"Hi Mary," I responded. "Life plays funny tricks, doesn't it?"

Right then was the first of the many times that that little blond girl has surprised me.

"O I dont know about that," she said, quite serious now. "I've often thought that very little happens *by accident*. In the little time I've been around I've seen too many things that make real patterns. No, I honestly believe there's a plan somewhere. Maybe we ourselves have had at least a little part in making it. It could be, we're here on earth for the chance to learn, and to grow up a little."

I took a deep breath. I had no answer for that except a slow, emphatic nod. Then a way came to me, a way to get into the whole matter, obvious enough now yet at the moment it was like a flash of light.

"Tell me, please," I said, "and believe me there's a point to my question: Have you ever cared at all about reading Science Fiction?"

121

She grinned again at that, and I think she blushed a little. Whatever it was, there was more color in her face.

"Yes," she said, nodding, "as a matter of fact it's one of my favorite vices. I generally keep it dark because I come of a family that takes its literature seriously. Mind you, the mechanized horror stuff, and the space-demon fantasies haven't ever appealed to me. But things like journeys to other planets, C. S. Lewis for instance, though you couldn't really call him Science Fiction, and time travel. . . ."

She stopped in the middle of her train of ideas, interrupting herself.

"It seems to me," she went on in a different tone of voice, "I seem to remember something about that just in the time before I went to sleep. You see, Daddy teaches at M.I.T., and there was some hush-hush talk about an experimental machine and someone going to try to get back in time."

So, all in the third person I told her the story, just about as it had broken in the papers and then been described in some of the better periodicals. Mary was fascinated, and as far as I could see she was absorbed but utterly relaxed. So I was sure that so far this wasn't taxing her strength.

It was obvious that she didn't, even in her sub-conscious, connect me in any way with what I'd said. So I had to believe it when she told me that she'd "always been drawn to Ancient Egypt," devoured all that she could read about it and somehow felt a kinship with that time.

I told her that I had, too.

"Then there's at least one thing we have in common," she said, smiling a little, and held her hand out to me. We shook hands semi-formally like ship-board acquaintances that have just introduced themselves. But somehow, we didn't let go again. Still clasping her hand as firmly as she held mine, I seated myself, very gently, on the edge of her bed.

"Frankly," she went on, "you've just frightened me a little with these things about Egypt, and that annoyed me. Because I like you, very very much, and I don't see any reason to be frightened. And of course, aside from all that, I'm ever so grateful. Dr. Bill told me of what you'd done for me.

"I was wondering. . . . He told me you'd had a loss, somebody you'd loved very much. I was just wondering," she said this a little dreamily, as if from far-away places in her being, "would you want to tell me about her?"

With that, I didn't "take a plunge," it was rather that the deep waters flooded over me.

I was careful to keep my voice low, and, I think, casual and relaxed. I told her I'd been the one who had made that journey back in time. She looked a little startled, but in no wise shocked. It seemed obvious that she herself still felt no connection with the matter.

"Why then," she said, and her voice had the comforting tenderness of Woman, no matter if at the moment Woman speaks as mother, bride or child, "of course Nutka is the one you've lost. You didn't speak so much of her in telling me the story, but before I knew that the man was you I'd sensed that there was something had grown up between them that was far more than any casual just 'being together' of two people."

I had to go on from there, I couldn't leave it now.

"Didn't Dr. Bill tell you," I asked her, still in a low tone, "did he tell you the words I used to wake you with?"

She shook her head wonderingly. I intoned the words again, with all the love in them that I'd felt for Nutka.

"Ra em Pet."

"Weben?" she answered, and I'll swear it was with Nutka's very intonation.

She caught herself then, with a sharply indrawn breath.

"How could I? I know no Egyptian. I'd always meant to look into the language, books about it, but Joe, I never did. I never did."

Then she burst into weeping. I held her close. She went on being racked with sobs. I pressed the call for Bill and he came in a few seconds later nodded at me and said "Don't worry."

As he was mixing something for her in a glass of water I tried, for Mary's sake, to disengage myself.

Mary moaned "No, don't go, Joe. Please don't go."

I looked at Bill. He shook his head emphatically. So I stayed, and gently cradled her in my arms. Very soon she was asleep, from what he'd given her to drink. The doctor listened to her breathing. It was quiet, even and deep breathing. The first real smile, the first relaxed smile I'd seen him wear in a long while was on his face.

"That's a true sleep, Joe. You can lay her down now. I want her warmly covered. We're out of the woods."

"Out of the woods," I murmured, echoing him, and rather hysterically, I think, in my tone. "It may seem that way to you. I'm terrified. I don't want to spoil *another* life for someone."

He went on smiling.

"You're too close to it to be able to believe me, but I tell you it's going to be good, good, good, and for the good in every way. Don't ask me how I know that, but I do. Just rarely, doctors do have intuition."

There was no answer to that one, though I couldn't believe him. And in the back of my mind I knew that Dr. X wasn't one for soothing syrup. And yet . . . I wished I *could* believe him.

I managed, as people somehow will, to get through the next twenty-four hours. I found myself again in that upstairs, corner room.

Mary greeted me shyly, or rather, she seemed shy to me. I tried to make casual conversation. It got nowhere and we both were miserable.

Finally she held out both arms, and asked me to kiss her. A long time later she sighed, and settled back.

"We know, don't we?" she murmured then. "And we can't think of anything to say because there's nothing to be said.

"Well, at least my family, being a wonderful kind of family, wont fuss about our getting married. We'll just take it on from there. And we'll be married very soon. I'm saying this for you, because I do think I know how you feel, and that you wouldn't because you, somehow couldn't.

"That *is* what you want too, isn't it?"

I nodded, and she answered me by holding out her arms again.

I had intended to take this story still further. Yet, going back over it this far I've come to the conclusion that it really has been told.

We are most happy together. For our work, we are doing something that could only be defined as ethnological research. While we try to be careful not to offend the scientists' mores, what it amounts to is something along the lines of part of Heyerdahl's work.

We go out to less-visited places on this earth and live a fair while among one or another of the so-called "primitive peoples." We try, by *living into* their thoughts and ways and feelings, to sense what lives on in them from older times. And often, then, they meet us with their confidence—which we never abuse. But we have been able to learn, and get evidence for, a lot of that which lies behind their ancient folkways.

Our professor friends are pleased, and say we are making genuine contributions. For this, we are glad. But we both feel that perhaps the contribution lies more in the fact that various old facets of the realities that never do change will not become entirely lost to the world in the on-sweep of Western Civilization. In a sense it is rather like the archaeology being practiced in many parts of our American West where dam constructions successively flood vast areas lived in long ages ago by earlier Americans. We feel that we must salvage what we can.

Everywhere we find the same core of the underlying truths: Man's origin out of the Divine, his dwelling here on earth to learn and grow. His eventual Destiny, far off yet but being helped always where help is needed, to return after many Earth Ages again to the Divine, but then to work creatively out of the love born of freedom, in the shaping of new worlds when there shall be "a new Heaven and a new Earth."

Of our personal life I shall say very little, although Mary —knowing why I have attempted this book, has given me carte blanche.

I have said that our happiness together is unsurpassable. And it continues, and will be until we die. This we both know, although we could not tell you why. We are both a little older than we were back in those other times—I too, although I am clothed in the same body while her garment has been changed. So; being a little wiser, we find fulfilment in the living moment. This goes beyond the bodily, which is wondrous in itself. It lives in our souls and penetrates to that in each of us that says "I" to itself.

It becomes true even in pain and disappointment, and I must state it clearly that we have plenty of both, as well as surpassing joys. And it remains true in all of the moments of gladness, be this gladness in one another, in a task we do, or in the glorious colors of sunrise and sunset when the true Gods still walk abroad and men can, if they will, still see the sheen of their garments.

And each night, as it comes on, is the most wonderful of all. We look up into it together for we know that in it there are not only the groupings of the stars. Across and through that seeming darkness there is flowing, weaving, always, the living light of the Sun, needing only a created object to reflect it into visibility.